DOCTOR WHO
DEATH TO THE DALEKS

DOCTOR WHO
DEATH TO THE DALEKS

Based on the BBC television serial *Death to the Daleks* by Terry Nation by arrangement with the British Broadcasting Corporation

TERRANCE DICKS

A TARGET BOOK
Published by
the Paperback Division of
W. H. ALLEN & Co. Ltd

A Target Book

Published in 1978
by the Paperback Division of W. H. Allen & Co. Ltd
A Howard & Wyndham Company
44 Hill Street, London W1X 8LB

Text of book copyright © 1978 by Terrance Dicks
and Terry Nation
'Doctor Who' series copyright © 1978 by the
British Broadcasting Corporation
Daleks created by Terry Nation

Third impression 1980

Printed in Great Britain by
Richard Clay (The Chaucer Press) Ltd, Bungay, Suffolk

ISBN 0 426 20042 X

Contents

Prologue

He was a dead man running.

He ran blindly, desperately through the swirling green fog, deep, sobbing breaths rasping into his tortured lungs. He knew there was little hope. Somehow he had been separated from the others in the ambush, and now his enemies were hunting him. Without checking his run, he glanced back over his shoulder. Shadowy figures were flitting through the dunes behind him.

His foot slipped on a loose rock and he pitched forward on to his face. He rolled over, scrambled to his feet and ran on, snatching another quick look behind him. This time he saw nothing, but he knew they were all around him, herding him across the dunes like a hunted beast. As he ran, confused memories flashed through his mind. Selection for this all-important mission, farewells to family and friends on Earth, the landing on this isolated hell-planet. And then—disaster. A superbly-equipped expedition, from one of the most advanced cultures in the galaxy, suddenly and utterly helpless.

He reached a small, stagnant pool, stopped to get his bearings—and a black-cloaked, hooded figure rose up before him like a ghost. He turned aside—and another appeared, barring his path. He swung round. More silent figures had appeared behind him.

He snatched the blaster from his belt and glared defiantly around him. The weapon was useless on this planet, but if one of them came close enough, he could use it as a club.

There was a sudden blur of movement from one of the silent figures and he felt a blow over the heart. It felt no worse than a heavy punch, but when he looked down there was an arrow jutting from his chest. More arrows thudded into his body and he staggered back, falling with a splash into the little pool. As its darkness swallowed him, his last, bitter thought was that he had failed. His entire mission had failed, and because of that failure, untold millions would die a hideous death . . .

I

Death of a TARDIS

The police box, which was not a police box at all, sped through that mysterious void where space and time are one. Inside the impossibly large control room a tall, white-haired man with a deeply-lined, young-old face was making a few final adjustments to the instruments. Despite the ultra-modern nature of his surroundings, he was dressed with old-fashioned elegance, in narrow trousers, velvet smoking jacket and ruffled shirt.

A door opened and an attractive, dark haired girl appeared. She wore an abbreviated beach robe, over a twentieth century bathing costume, and carried a big, striped beach bag. 'It's all in here, Doctor. Sun glasses, sun lotion, water-wings . . .'

The Doctor smiled. 'You won't need water-wings, Sarah.'

'Oh yes I will. You said we were going swimming . . .'

'You can't sink on Florana.'

'I can sink anywhere,' said Sarah pessimistically. 'I need a life-jacket in my bath.'

'The water on Florana is effervescent. The bubbles support you.'

'Sounds like swimming in a glass of health salts.'

The Doctor was in great good humour. 'All right, Sarah, all right. Just wait till you've seen Florana. It's the most beautiful holiday planet in the galaxy.'

Sarah felt contrite. It seemed unfair to be so suspicious when the Doctor was in such a holiday mood. But somehow she just couldn't help wondering if the Doctor's lavish promises about their destination were really going to be fulfilled. During her relatively brief acquaintance with the Doctor, the TARDIS had taken her to a particularly violent era of England's medieval past, and to a London mysteriously infested with dinosaurs.

The Doctor had assured her that this time everything would be different. To make up for these terrifying experiences he was taking her to the most beautiful, the most peaceful planet in the galaxy.

She noticed that a red light was flashing on the TARDIS control console. Other lights began to flicker, and needles on the instrument-dials were oscillating wildly. She looked at the Doctor, but he was staring blissfully into space, still summoning up the beauties of Florana. 'I always come away from those long golden beaches feeling a hundred years younger . . .'

'Doctor . . .'

'And the beauty of Florana is that unlike your own little planet it hasn't yet been spoiled by—'

'Doctor, should that red light be flashing like that? *And* all those others?'

The Doctor swung round, and saw alarm signals registering all over the TARDIS console. He dashed frantically around the console, adjusting controls. A fuse blew with a crackle of sparks and a puff of smoke. The lights in the control room went dim.

Sarah was frankly terrified. 'What is it, Doctor, what's happening?'

'There seems to be a major power failure. Hang on,

I'll cut in the emergency circuits.' The Doctor pulled a lever and all at once everything returned to normal. The main lights came up again, the warning lights went out. 'That's a relief,' said the Doctor. 'If the emergency units hadn't worked, we'd have been in real trouble.'

The main lights began to fade, and the emergency signals on the console started flickering once more.

'It's happening again,' said Sarah. 'Do something, Doctor!'

The Doctor was leaning over the controls, frowning in concentration. For the TARDIS to fail in this way meant only one thing. Some outside force was operating against it. A sudden fierce jolt made him clutch the console for support, and sent Sarah staggering. 'What's happened, Doctor?'

'I can tell you one thing, Sarah. We've landed.' He pointed to the centre column which rose and fell steadily while the TARDIS was in flight. It was motionless.

One by one the warning lights on the TARDIS console started to go out, and the indicator needles on the dials crept back towards zero. The main lights grew dimmer and dimmer, and there was an uncanny silence. 'It's as if the TARDIS is dying,' whispered Sarah.

'I'd better try the scanner—while there's still enough power to operate it,' said the Doctor. He threw the switch, and the scanner screen lit up. The picture was dim and fuzzy and all it showed them was sand dunes and swirling green fog. Slowly the picture faded and the scanner screen went black. 'Fascinating,' murmured the Doctor.

'What's so fascinating about fog?'

'Perhaps that fog is what's putting the TARDIS out of action.'

The concealed lights in the TARDIS ceiling began going out one by one. Section after section of the TARDIS was plunged into darkness. Finally one central light-source was left, bathing the console, the Doctor and Sarah in a little circle of light. Then it too began to fade.

'Don't you have any other emergency power source?' asked Sarah.

'Yes, of course. I'll switch over to the back-up system.' He threw a switch and the lights came up again. Sarah smiled with relief—but not for long. Slowly the lights began to fade.

'Dud battery?' suggested Sarah nervously.

'Hardly. Listen.'

'I can't hear anything.'

'Exactly. Neither can I. Nothing at all. Not a click or a tick. Nothing. The TARDIS is a living thing, hundreds of complex instruments, working all the time. It's energy sources are perpetual—never stop.'

'Well, they have now. Everything's completely dead.'

'It's just as you said. The TARDIS is dying.' The Doctor looked around the control room. It was almost completely dark now, just the faintest of glimmers from the central light. 'Sarah, look in that locker over there. I think there should be a torch on the upper shelf.'

Sarah opened the locker and groped inside. She took out an enormous torch, the heavy industrial kind covered in black rubber. She switched it on and a beam of bright light illuminated the console. Sarah felt better immediately—until the beam of the torch began slowly fading. In a matter of seconds it had died completely and the darkness returned.

The Doctor was hunting inside another locker. He emerged carrying a large, old-fashioned lamp, the sort coal miners used to use. Sarah managed a smile. 'Don't tell me—you're going to rub it and produce a genie!'

The Doctor held the lamp to his ear and shook it. 'On the contrary, I'm going to cast some light on our situation!' He took a box of old-fashioned sulphur matches from the locker, struck one and lit the lamp. A pool of soft yellow light bathed the area around them.

Sarah breathed a sigh of relief. 'Well, hooray for good old-fashioned oil!'

The Doctor turned up the wick and the light grew brighter. 'That's better. Now, we'd better go outside and find out where we are.'

Sarah gave him a sceptical look. 'I bet it isn't Florana!'

He passed her the lantern. 'Hold this a minute, will you? The door controls won't be working. I'll have to open them manually.' He went to a tool locker in the base of the control console and took out an iron lever, rather like the starting handle of an old-fashioned car. Crossing to the doors, the Doctor slipped the handle into a wall socket and began to turn it. Slowly the doors started to open, and green fog drifted into the room. It seemed to chill the air. Sarah shivered inside her beach robe. The Doctor opened the door a little wider and went outside. Nervously Sarah followed.

There was little enough to see. The TARDIS seemed to have landed in the middle of sand dunes—their low rounded shapes stretched away into the greenish fog.

Coarse grey sand crunched underfoot as they moved cautiously away from the TARDIS. Sarah shivered. 'It's so cold . . .'

'Come on,' said the Doctor. 'Let's take a look around.' They walked on through the dunes for quite some time. Suddenly Sarah jumped back in terror as a menacing black figure loomed up out of the fog.

The Doctor held her arm. 'All right, Sarah, it's only a rock.' It was a kind of monolith, a fantastically-carved shape in black stone. He went to examine it more closely. 'It could be some kind of statue or even some form of native life that became petrified long ago.'

'I was pretty close to being petrified myself!'

The Doctor picked up a handful of the coarse gravel-like sand and rubbed it thoughtfully between his fingers. 'This part of the planet seems quite dead, I doubt if anything has grown here for centuries.'

'Well, unless you're planning to settle down here and raise lettuce, that doesn't seem too important.'

The Doctor ignored her. 'If the rest of the place is like this, then the whole planet may be completely lifeless.'

'Look, Doctor, we're not on some kind of scientific study expedition. All we want to do is get away from here.'

'I quite agree. But to leave this planet, we must first understand it.'

'Why?'

'Think! Some power emanating from this planet has drained the TARDIS's energy banks. Now, either it's a natural phenomenon or—'

'Somebody or something is doing it deliberately.'

The Doctor nodded like some teacher whose pupil has finally come up with the answer. 'Exactly.'

'Well, now we've got that settled, can't you just fix the TARDIS and clear out?'

'You're missing the point, Sarah. The trouble isn't *in* the TARDIS. To get away from here we've got to find whatever's blocking our energy-sources and neutralise it.'

'And how do we do that?'

'For the moment, I haven't the slightest idea.'

'But unless we *can* do it, we're trapped? Stuck here forever?'

'That's right,' said the Doctor cheerfully. 'So we'd better get busy.'

'What do we do first?'

'We start by investigating the immediate area.'

'All right,' said Sarah bravely. She shivered again, looking at the shadowy dunes shrouded in green fog. It was bitterly cold. 'I'm not exactly dressed for this climate though, am I?'

'What?' The Doctor realised Sarah was still in bathing costume and beach robe, ready for the promised beaches of Florana. 'For goodness sakes, girl, go and get on something warm.'

'All right. Don't go away, Doctor, will you?'

The Doctor was absorbed in examining the black monolith with his oil-lamp. Sarah gave him a despairing look, and hurried off towards the TARDIS.

The Doctor went on with his examination. The monolith could be of natural origin. It was perfectly possible that swirling sand storms had gradually carved the rock pillar into its present fantastic shape. Or was it a statue of some kind, worn away by the passage of time? Then there was the other theory he'd mentioned to Sarah. Perhaps it was some creature of the planet, dead for untold thousands of years, petrified into its present form. Perhaps it had once been one of the planet's intelligent life-forms.

Absorbed in his speculations, the Doctor didn't notice that black-robed figures had appeared silently out of the fog. They began stalking slowly towards him . . .

2

The Ambush

Sarah slipped through the half-open door of the
TARDIS and groped her way to the wardrobe locker.
Working by touch she began sorting out some clothes.
Trousers, a heavy sweater, some comfortable walking
shoes and a nice warm jacket . . . Hurriedly she started
to change.

The Doctor went on examining the monolith, while
behind him black-robed shapes edged ever closer . . .

Outside the TARDIS Sarah looked fearfully around.
The fog-shadowed dunes looked as sinister as ever, but
now she felt better equipped to cope with its unknown
dangers. You could hardly be expected to tackle some
alien monstrosity when you were wearing a bathing
suit. She looked for the glow of the Doctor's lantern, but
saw only blackness and swirling fog.

'Doctor!' she called. No reply. 'Doctor! Are you
there?' Still the silence. Nervously Sarah began hurrying in the direction of the stone pillar.

(As she hurried off a black-clad shape slipped from
behind the TARDIS and stood poised, looking after
her. It hovered as if about to attack, then turned,

moving silently towards the still-open TARDIS door.)

Sarah was beginning to fear that she'd missed her way. There was no sign of the Doctor. She couldn't even see the monolith. Hoping desperately that the Doctor wasn't too far away Sarah called, 'Doctor? Doctor, I'm lost. Where are you?' Silence. She heard a faint scuttling sound behind her and turned in alarm, but there was nothing to be seen. Only the rolling sand dunes and the swirling fog.

In sudden panic Sarah started to run, and blundered straight into something that grabbed at her. She screamed and pulled away, but it was only a scrubby thorn-bush that had caught on her jacket. Freeing herself, Sarah gazed round in panic—and caught a sudden glimpse of a tall figure carrying an oil lamp. With a sob of relief she ran up to it—then stopped in disappointment. It wasn't the Doctor at all. It was the statue-like rock where she'd last seen him. The oil lamp was perched on a stone spur that stuck out like an arm.

'Doctor!' she shouted. 'Doctor, where are you?' There was no reply. She went up to the monolith and took down the lamp. It felt sticky to her touch and she looked closely at her fingers. They were smeared with blood.

Sarah dropped the lamp—which went out, leaving her in darkness. She stood for a moment, fighting down her panic. Should she go and look for the Doctor? In this foggy darkness she would be exposed and vulnerable to whatever enemy had attacked him. She decided to go back to the TARDIS and wait. She'd be safe there, and there was always a chance that the Doctor would come back to find her. If he didn't, she would go out and look for him when it got light.

Pausing a moment to get her bearings, she headed back towards the TARDIS.

As she hurried along, she heard strange noises all around her. At times she thought she saw black shapes flitting through the darkness. But she reached the TARDIS safely enough, and paused, sobbing for breath. Telling herself sternly not to make matters worse by imagining things, she went inside.

Back in the darkened control room, Sarah was angry with herself for not bringing the blood-smeared lamp. Now she'd have to try to find another one, and some more matches too. She paused for a moment by the door of the TARDIS, looking out over the sand dunes, half-hoping to see the Doctor hurrying towards her. But he was nowhere in sight. She heard movements from out in the fog, and realised she'd left the TARDIS door open. She went to the crank, still in its wall socket, and began to turn it. Slowly the door started to close. The crank was stiff and it took all Sarah's strength to move it. Absorbed in her task, she didn't see the tall black shape that rose from its hiding place behind the control panel ... A whisper of sudden movement caught her ear, and she turned to see a bat-like figure swooping down on her, eyes gleaming evilly beneath a monk-like hood.

Her hand was still on the crank-handle, and snatching it from its socket, she swung it in terror at the approaching shape. The iron handle thudded down on to the black hood. The creature gave a shrill cry of pain and flopped to the ground.

Sarah turned to run but thanks to her own efforts, the door was now closed again. Hurriedly she rammed the handle back in its socket and started winding it the other way.

As she turned the handle she kept a wary eye on the creature on the floor. To her horror she saw that it was stirring. She wound the handle faster and faster. Soon the door was open wide enough to get through. As she moved towards it, the creature came suddenly to life. Lunging towards her, it grabbed her ankle with a skinny claw. Sarah pulled the handle free, and smashed it down across the bony arm. With a shriek of pain it released her, and she slipped through the gap and out across the dunes.

As she ran desperately on, Sarah became aware that the darkness was no longer quite so thick. The fog was lifting, and in the sky above her were the first pale streaks of dawn.

The Doctor was being marched along a path between the dunes, escorted by two hooded black-robed figures. The one in front was dragging him along by a rope which formed a noose around his neck. The one behind was carrying a flaming torch.

The Doctor stumbled onwards, tugged on by a jerk on the rope whenever he slowed down. His head was slumped, he was bleeding from a cut on his forehead, and he moved like a man barely conscious. But in reality the Doctor wasn't nearly as badly off as he was making out. His strength was returning rapidly, and he was deliberately exaggerating his weakness in the hope of catching his captors off guard.

His mind went quickly back over his capture. Alerted by the faintest of noises he had looked up—and immediately the alien had pounced, claw-like hands seizing him by the throat. It was wiry and incredibly strong, but once over his surprise the Doctor reckoned he would have been able to deal with it. Indeed, he had already broken free—when another of the creatures had snatched up the brass lamp and aimed a savage blow at his head. The Doctor had caught a brief glimpse of gleaming eyes in a distorted face—then the heavy lamp had taken him across the forehead and he'd blacked out.

And now here he was, a captive of these hideous creatures. Presumably they were taking him back to their base. The Doctor was determined to break free before they arrived. He might be able to deal with two of the aliens but he didn't want to take on any more.

Choosing his moment, the Doctor gave a feeble groan, stumbled artistically, and collapsed on the path. The leading alien jerked savagely on the noose, but the Doctor didn't move. The one with the torch knelt beside the Doctor to examine him, shoving the burning torch towards his face. To its surprise, the alien saw that the Doctor's eyes were wide open and alert. A bony fist shot out with savage force, taking the alien under the chin, and it slumped back unconscious. Immediately the Doctor was on his feet. The second alien yanked on the noose, pulling him off-balance, but the Doctor grabbed the rope and snatched it from the alien's hand. With a screech of rage it rushed into the attack. Rolling over backwards the Doctor shot up both legs. The alien flew a surprising distance through the air and landed further down the rocky path with a thud that knocked it senseless. The Doctor got to his feet and pulled the noose from his neck. He tossed it aside, looked at his unconscious opponents with satisfaction and turned back the way he had come. The first thing to do was find Sarah. He only hoped she'd had the sense to wait in the TARDIS . . .

But Sarah was some way from the TARDIS by now, running across the dunes with no clear idea where she was going. At first it had been enough to get away from the flapping horror in the control room. But she was beginning to realise that she couldn't just run on indefinitely. She must stop and make a plan.

Ahead of her the dunes were rising sharply. It was light enough now for her to see that the dune area formed a kind of giant bowl—and she was coming to its edge. She toiled on up the slope wondering what lay on the other side of the steep rise—and froze as she heard swift, shuffling footsteps close behind her.

Not far away, the winds had scooped an overhanging ledge into the side of the nearest dune. Sarah left the path and flung herself down, rolling over and tucking herself beneath the ledge for cover.

She lay very still, doing her best to burrow her way into the sand. From her hiding place she saw two black-cloaked, hooded forms loping along the path towards her. They came nearer, nearer—and stopped. They held a brief, agitated conference. One of them turned and ran back down the path. The other hovered for a moment, and followed.

She waited until they were out of sight, then came out of her hiding place, trying to work out what had been happening. Clearly the creatures had been on her track—and equally clearly, they had been reluctant to go further up the path.

Sarah decided anywhere those hooded horrors wanted to keep away from was the right place for her. She began climbing up the steep track as fast as she could, and a few minutes later she stood on the crest of the rise. She stopped, eyes widening in amazement.

Ahead of her stretched a vast plain made of smooth level rock. It was as though someone had sliced off the top of a mountain with a giant cleaver. In the centre of this plateau there was a City. It was made of white, gleaming marble-like stone and its towers stretched upwards to the dark clouds that floated across the grey morning sky. The design was ultra-modern, all smooth level surfaces and squared off, geometrically regular shapes, with something of the towering majesty of the Aztec temples of Earth. Adjoining the City was an enormous tower, and at the top of this tower was a beacon. It pulsed in a steady, regular rhythm like some colossal lighthouse.

For some time Sarah stood there, gazing in awe. There was a civilisation on this planet after all. Perhaps the creature that had attacked her was merely one of the barbarians of this world, one of the savages who skulked outside the City without daring to approach. Only an advanced, ultra-civilised race could build a place such as this. Surely they would help her to rescue the Doctor, help to repair the TARDIS and send them on their way. Full of renewed hope, Sarah set off towards the City.

*

The Doctor meanwhile was trying to find his way back to the TARDIS. Unfortunately, the dunes looked much alike, and he had no idea how far, or indeed in what direction, his captors had dragged him while he was semi-conscious. Now he too had come to the edge of the dunes, to an area of wild broken country strewn with huge boulders, the lower slopes of the range of mountains that fringed the area. For a moment the Doctor considered turning back—he certainly hadn't come this way before. But if he did that he risked losing himself again. He decided to climb higher and get a general view of the area. With luck he might even be able to spot the TARDIS. He started to climb the rocky path ahead of him. The path rose steeply, and soon it was enclosed in high rock walls as it wound across the face of the mountain. The Doctor marched determinedly on. If he could scale that spur just ahead and look back the way he had come . . .

Suddenly he found that he had stopped, and was staring cautiously about him. It was as if his subconscious mind had spotted some danger and was trying to warn him. He studied the path ahead. There was no sound, no movement. Everything was normal. He took a few cautious paces forward, and stopped again. Stretching across the path, concealed under some loose brushwood, there was a rope. It was obviously designed to trip anyone coming along the path. He touched it with a cautious finger. It was taut, like a bow string. The ends disappeared into the shrubs on either side of the path.

The Doctor looked thoughtfully at the rope, and backed away. He picked up a football-sized rock and lobbed it hard along the path. As the rock hit the rope, there was a grinding sound from the hillside above, and a huge boulder smashed down on to the path—at exactly the point where a passer-by would have been standing when his foot touched the rope. The boulder rolled across the path and disappeared down the mountainside.

Crude, but effective, thought the Doctor, as the rumbling died away. He wondered what other traps were waiting for him—and suddenly someone jumped him from behind. At first the Doctor assumed that his black-cloaked enemies had caught up with him. Then he saw that the arm across his throat was clad in silvery-grey plastic-type material—and the knife that was stabbing towards his chest was made from a single piece of metal —a spaceman's knife. Interesting as this was, there were more urgent problems. The Doctor dug his chin into his chest to counter the stranglehold, grabbed his attacker's knife-wrist with both hands, swept a leg round his attacker's ankle and threw himself backwards. He crashed to the ground, his assailant beneath him. But the shock of the fall broke the Doctor's grip. The attacker rolled away, sprang to his feet and came into the attack, knife held low. As the knife flashed forward the Doctor grabbed desperately for the knife-wrist and caught it yet again. But the Doctor was still in an awkward crouch: his opponent was poised and determined and very strong. He loomed over the Doctor, blocking out the light. The knife came closer and closer to the Doctor's throat . . .

3

Expedition from Earth

A hand appeared, knocking the knife aside. Roughly the newcomer pulled the attacker away. 'All right, Galloway, that's enough. You can see he's not an Exxilon.'

The man called Galloway stepped back, the killing anger fading from his face. 'Aye, you're right. But it was all so quick. He sprung the trap, d'you see, and then we were fighting . . .'

The newcomer helped the Doctor to his feet. 'I'm sorry,' he said gruffly. 'We've had a pretty bad time on this planet. Quite a few of us have been killed. Dan Galloway here tends to attack first and ask questions afterwards. My name's Railton, by the way . . .'

Dusting himself down, the Doctor studied the two men. Galloway, the one who'd attacked him, was big and burly, with a barrel-chest and great hairy hands. The second man was considerably smaller and several years older, with thinning hair and a lined, careworn face. Both wore astronaut-type uniforms with military insignia, both had blasters and knives in their belts.

Galloway was carrying a bow, improvised, the Doctor noticed, from a flexible plastic rod. A plastic quiver filled with arrows of sharpened cane hung over his shoulder.

Rubbing his bruises, the Doctor said ruefully, 'I'm the Doctor. I can understand how you feel, gentlemen. I was attacked myself as soon as I arrived. Perhaps you can tell me—'

Galloway was looking back down the path. 'Something moving,' he whispered urgently. 'Getting closer.'

Railton tensed. The Doctor listened. From around the bend of the path came a faint shuffling sound. Railton said urgently, 'You'd better come back to base with us. We can talk safely there.'

Galloway was already scrambling over the rocks, moving away from the path. Railton set off after him and the Doctor followed. Soon all three had disappeared amongst the tumbled rocks.

Minutes later a black-cloaked figure appeared. Others followed. They stood for a moment, almost as if sniffing the air, then set off over the rocks after their prey.

Galloway led the way over the broken ground at a terrific pace. He doubled back in a wide loop and soon they were moving along the edge of a low cliff at a point where the rocks bordered the dunes. Galloway made for a shallow niche in the rock face, and the Doctor saw that a small plastic survival dome had been erected against the base of the cliff. It was a good position, protected from above by the overhang of the cliff, shielded on each side by the arms of the V-shaped niche. As they headed for the dome, a man with a bow and arrow seemed to rise out of the ground. The Doctor looked closer and saw that a protective trench had been dug just in front of them.

At the sight of the Doctor's companions, the sentry lowered his bow and gave a cheerful grin. He was considerably younger than the other two with brown hair and a round cheerful face.

Railton returned the wave. 'All right, Peter, it's only us. We've got a visitor, but he's quite friendly.'

'We hope!' muttered Galloway. He was still keeping a wary eye on the Doctor, his hand close to the hilt of his knife.

Railton led the way into the dome, slapping the sentry on the shoulder as he went by. 'Keep a sharp look out, Peter. Dan heard some movement back there.'

Peter gave a quick salute. 'Aye, aye, sir.' He sank back into his trench, eyes scanning the broken ground ahead.

The Doctor looked round the dome. He was in a large circular chamber, divided into different sections. There were sleeping bags against the wall, and in the central area there was a scattered pile of partially-unpacked crates which appeared to contain some kind of mining equipment. Near the crates was an assortment of improvised weapons—clubs, spears, slingshots, bows and arrows, made partly from steel and plastic, partly from wood and rock.

On the far side of the dome screens had been set up forming a little cubicle. Inside it, on a makeshift bed, lay a heavily bandaged man. A young woman was kneeling beside him, tucking an aerofoil space blanket into place. She straightened up at the sight of the others, brushing back fair hair from her forehead. 'Who's this? Did you find Jack?'

Railton didn't reply, and there was an awkward silence. Then Galloway said brutally, 'Aye, we found him, right enough. Floating in one of the pools, stuck full of arrows like a hedgehog.'

The young woman gave a gasp of horror and Railton said gently, 'We buried him out there, Jill. It seemed best.'

The girl nodded, absorbing the shock. She looked at the Doctor. 'And who's this then?'

Galloway said. 'He calls himself the Doctor. We found him, out there.'

'This is Jill Tarrant, Doctor,' said Railton. 'She's our mining engineer. The lad on guard outside is Peter Hamilton.'

'There are just the five of you then?'

'There used to be ten,' said Galloway bleakly. 'Two were killed in that first ambush. Three more have been picked off since.'

Railton looked at the man on the bed. He was dozing uneasily. 'This is Commander Stewart, the leader of our expedition. He was wounded in the first ambush.'

'Commander? You're a military expedition then?'

'Mixed,' said Railton. 'Miss Tarrant and I are scientists. The rest are all M.S.C.'

The Doctor frowned. 'M.S.C.?'

'Marine Space Corps,' said Galloway. 'You've plenty of questions, Doctor. Now maybe you'll tell us something about yourself? Where do you come from? And where were you heading when I jumped you?'

'Back to the TARDIS—my space-ship.' The Doctor gave a brief account of his arrival on the planet, the mysterious power failure, and the ambush which had separated him from Sarah. 'I only hope she had the sense to stay in the ship,' he concluded. 'But I'm afraid

Sarah's inclined to be headstrong. By now she's probably out looking for me.'

'Then she's probably dead by now,' said Galloway.

The Doctor gave him a frown, and Railton said, 'She *might* still be all right, Doctor, as long as she's careful. The Exxilons are mainly night creatures.'

'Exxilons? I take it those are the inhabitants of this planet—the unfriendly gentlemen in the cloaks and hoods?'

Railton nodded. 'They usually keep out of sight in the day time. Maybe they won't find her.'

'Just as long as she doesn't go near the forbidden city,' added Jill. 'That's guarded day and night.'

Gloomily Galloway said, 'Aye, that's right. Anyone they catch nearby—that's their lot.' He made a slashing gesture.

'We've seen Exxilon prisoners being taken from near the City into a big cavern where most of them live,' said Jill. 'We're not sure, but we think they're sacrificed.'

The Doctor felt somewhat overwhelmed with all this new information. But it was vital that he absorb it as quickly as possible. The more he knew about the planet, the better his chances of finding Sarah, and of finally escaping from it altogether. He looked round at the others. 'I've only just arrived on this singularly unpleasant planet, and you've obviously been here for some time. I'd be very much obliged if you'd tell me all you can . . .

Sarah moved on across the rocky plateau. The sun was up by now, larger and closer than the sun of Earth. It blazed down at her from a coppery sky, and reflected upwards from the bare rocks. She could feel their heat through the soles of her shoes. Hot, tired and thirsty, Sarah stumbled on. Perhaps the City would be a kind of Arabian Nights palace, she thought. There would be cool courtyards with gently splashing fountains, and white-robed attendants with long cool drinks in golden goblets . . .

The City was very close now. Its white buildings rose up and up, blotting out the sky. Sarah paused to look again. There was something uncanny about the City, for all its beauty. There seemed to be no windows, no gates or doors. It was as if the City was blind.

Sarah hurried on. The last stretch of baking rock seemed endless, but she reached the walls of the City at last. White, smooth and unbroken they towered high above her, stretching away on either side as far as she could see.

Sarah went right up to the wall, and examined it curiously. At this close range she could see that it was made of enormous blocks, with only the finest of lines to mark the place where one block joined another. The wall was so bright and clean that it might have been built just a few hours ago. There was no dirt or dust, no sign of ageing or wear. Here and there elaborate patterns were cut into the wall. Sarah reached out and touched one of the patterns in front of her. The block on which it was carved was smooth and warm—and it *tingled*. Sarah snatched her hand away. The wall seemed to carry a mild electric charge. Perhaps that was what repelled the dirt—a kind of self-cleaning device. The people who had built this City must be very advanced indeed. She wished they'd been a bit more generous in the matter of gates and doors.

There was something else strange about the wall—a sound, a faint electronic hum. It was as though the entire City was somehow alive. She reached out and touched the wall again and heard a guttural snarl of anger.

Sarah whirled round. A group of black-cloaked, black-hooded figures had appeared behind her. She looked round for escape but she was surrounded. She backed away fearfully, but the wall of the City was behind her, cutting off her escape.

Bony hands outstretched, the horrifying nightmare figures advanced . . .

4

The Deadly Arrivals

Munching on a tube of food concentrate, and washing it down with water from a plastic bulb, the Doctor listened to Railton's account of the planet Exxilon and its strange inhabitants. The planet itself was bleak and barren, consisting mainly of sand dunes, rocks and deserts, with little vegetation or animal life. It was freezing cold and foggy at night, almost unbearably hot by day. Exxilon was a very old planet, with most of its resources drained and exhausted. It was Railton's theory that the planet had once been the home of some super-race which had since died out, or perhaps moved on to some other world.

Certainly, the present-day Exxilons were no more than ferocious savages. They had no civilisation, no machinery of any kind, only the simplest of weapons and tools. They appeared to live in a vast network of caves which honeycombed the planet, lurking underground by day, and coming out mainly at night. They were fiercely hostile, refusing all attempts at friendly contact, and attacking all strangers on sight. 'They could never have built anything like the City,' concluded Railton.

The Doctor finished his food-cube, wondering why no one ever managed to make the wretched things taste pleasant. 'This City you keep talking about . . . what does it look like?'

Railton said, 'Pass me the visual file, Jill. We've got some satellite pictures here, Doctor.' He passed a set of photographs across to the Doctor.

The Doctor studied them. Aerial views of miles of rocky terrain, with an occasional lake or pool. Dried-up rivers, and a kind of inland sea. Magnified shots that showed bands of black-robed figures scuttling across the face of the planet, ducking into cave mouths to hide. And finally the City, white, gleaming, enormous, towering into the coppery sky, the great tower with its beacon built on to its side. 'It seems to be the only building complex on the planet,' said Railton. 'It's bigger than a hundred ordinary cities. It's a fantastic place. It must have been built thousands of years ago, yet it still looks brand new.'

The Doctor studied the photographs. 'Fantastic, certainly. Have you ever been inside?'

Railton shook his head. 'We tried, but there doesn't seem to be any way in.'

'Not that we had very much time to look for one,' said Galloway. 'The Exxilons attacked as soon as we went near the place. We barely got away from there alive.'

The Doctor closed the file and handed it back. 'And what about your other problems? Forgive me for saying so, but your expedition seems to be in a pretty bad way.'

Railton nodded in gloomy agreement. 'We had a similar experience to your own, Doctor. As soon as we got close to Exxilon we had a total malfunction on all

34

instruments. We managed to touch down without damaging the ship—but we can't take off again.'

Galloway exploded. 'So we're stuck here on this stinking planet.' He tapped the blaster in his belt. 'Our weapons are as useless as the ship—and the Exxilons are picking us off one by one.'

'Why did you come here in the first place?' The Doctor looked at the scattered crates of equipment. 'Some kind of mining operation, I take it?'

Jill Tarrant said, 'We came for the Parrinium.' She looked at the Doctor as if that explained everything.

The Doctor was puzzled. 'Parrinium?'

'It's a mineral, Doctor, a kind of trace element. On most planets it's so rare that it's absolutely priceless. Then a detector satellite did a fly-past on this planet and found huge surface deposits. It's as common here as salt.'

'Forgive me, but what do you want it for?'

By now all three were staring at him in utter astonishment. 'Where have you been hiding, man?' asked Galloway.

'Oh, here and there, one place and another,' said the Doctor apologetically. 'I'm afraid I've been a little out of touch.'

Jill Tarrant's face was grave. 'Earth's colonies on the outer worlds are being ravaged by a terrible disease. A kind of space plague. No one knows where it came from or how it started, but the colonists are dying in their thousands. Millions more will die unless we help them— and every hour we're stuck on this planet the death roll is mounting.'

'Parrinium can cure this disease?'

35

'Completely. It cures, and it gives immunity. But we need it in quantity, and we need it fast. Unless it's delivered within a month it will be too late. We managed to get an emergency message out before the power failed. We asked them to send a relief ship.'

'The message never arrived,' said Galloway. 'If it had, we'd have had help by now.'

The Doctor said thoughtfully, 'Then we must act on the assumption that none is coming, and help ourselves. The first thing to do is to find out what's causing the power drain. My theory is that it's something to do with that City and its beacon. As soon as I've found Sarah we'll mount a joint expedition . . .'

Galloway was bristling with anger. 'Now hold on a minute. What gives you the right to make plans for us?'

'My concern for those dying millions,' said the Doctor crisply. 'Not to mention our own lives. You haven't been doing too well so far, have you?'

Railton sighed. 'I'm afraid that's true, Doctor. Personally I'd be happy to join forces.'

Galloway jabbed a thumb at the wounded man on the bed. 'Commander Stewart's still alive, isn't he? Well, I take my orders from him!—and no-one else.'

'I'm not talking about giving orders,' snapped the Doctor. 'I'm talking about co-operation—and about survival. So you'd better—' He broke off suddenly. 'Listen!' A faint droning sound was coming from high overhead.

Peter Hamilton dashed into the dome, almost incoherent with excitement. 'The relief ship,' he spluttered. 'It's here!'

They all ran outside the dome, and stared up at the sky. 'Did you see it, Peter?' asked Railton.

36

'No ... I heard it though. Up there in the heat haze ... over to the north, I think.'

'Probably making a spiral descent,' said Galloway excitedly. 'We should hear her again in a moment.'

Sure enough, a few minutes later, the low droning returned. It grew louder, and louder. 'Here she comes,' shouted Jill. High above them a gleaming metal shape flashed out of the clouds, then disappeared into the haze.

Peter Hamilton was on top of the nearest boulder. 'I can see her,' he shouted. 'They're landing in the next valley. Come on!' He set off across the rocks at a run, and the others followed. Caught up in the general excitement, the Doctor followed.

As the little group disappeared, two black-robed figures slipped from behind a nearby rock. Stealthily the Exxilons crept towards the dome.

Commander Stewart twisted and turned in fever-ridden sleep. The pain from his wounds, and above all his concern for his vital mission, fought with the drugs he had been given, and dragged him back to uneasy wakefulness. He licked dry lips and croaked 'Water ... water ...' A shadow fell over him, and he opened his eyes. Two black-clad figures loomed above him. Too weak to scream, Commander Stewart watched help-lessly as they swooped down towards him, blotting out the light.

One of her captors snatched the blindfold from her eyes, and for a moment Sarah thought she was in church. An arched roof rose high above her head, a choking smell of incense caught at her throat and the air was full of a deep sonorous chanting.

Her vision cleared and she gazed dazedly around her. She was in a huge cave, not a church, though its roof rose as high as that of any cathedral. It was lit by flaring torches, set at intervals round the rocky walls, and it was crowded with black-robed figures.

At the far side of the cavern, opposite what looked like a tunnel entrance, was a low stone altar. The guards dragged Sarah towards it. Now she was at close quarters with her captors, Sarah could see the faces beneath their hoods. The sight did nothing to reassure her. Although they were more or less humanoid, the faces were brutal, misshapen, degenerate, with loose mouths, flat noses and small close-set eyes glinting evilly. She could feel the pressure of fear and hatred as the crowd pressed close around her.

There was a space before the altar, and the guards thrust Sarah into the middle of it and stepped back. Behind the altar, one of the aliens stood on a raised platform. His bestial face was old and wrinkled, his robe was of finer quality than the others, and a necklace of barbaric ornaments glinted around his neck. He pointed a long skinny finger at Sarah and began to speak.

Sarah's mind went back to the fantasy of being in church. In a way it was true, she realised. She was in a kind of church, a temple of whatever religion these strange beings followed. And now the vicar was delivering his sermon.

Although she couldn't make out the words, the alien priest's tone and gestures made it clear what he was saying. She was being accused of some terrible crime. The high priest's speech drew angry roars of assent from the crowd. The priest's tone changed. His voice became deeper, graver, as if sentence was being pronounced. He pointed to Sarah, to the altar, and puzzlingly, to the tunnel entrance that lay just behind it.

Two alien priests came forward, carrying a kind of loose cloak ornamented with strange symbols. They draped the garment over Sarah's shoulders, seized her arms, and began dragging her towards the altar. All at once Sarah realised what was happening. She was going to be sacrificed! She began struggling wildly as they dragged her towards the altar.

Hamilton led the little party across the rocky hills. They moved quickly, pressing hopefully onwards, charged with new energy by their excitement. The Doctor, bringing up the rear, couldn't help feeling that all this optimism was a bit excessive. This second expedition would still have to overcome the problems faced by the first. But he could understand their relief now that they were no longer alone, their delight at the prospect of seeing faces from home.

They struggled to the top of a rise. Peter Hamilton pointed. 'Look, there it is!'

The space ship was just settling down to land in the centre of the rocky plain ahead of them, the flames of its retro-rockets dying away. Clouds of smoke and dust rose up around it, obscuring the shape.

'Come on!' shouted Jill and began running down the other side of the hill. The others followed.

By the time they reached the ship the smoke had

drifted away. It sat gleaming in the centre of the barren plain, the basic flying-saucer shape common to most interstellar craft. Peter Hamilton stared at it in puzzlement, and turned to Railton. 'It doesn't look much like an Earth ship to me, sir.'

Galloway said, 'It's maybe some new experimental model—that new Z-47 they've been planning.' But there was no conviction in his voice.

Railton mopped the sweat from his forehead. 'She's not a Space Corps craft,' he said slowly.

The Doctor said nothing. He stood gazing thoughtfully up at the ship.

'What do you think, Doctor?' asked Railton.

'I think we'll know soon enough.'

Galloway stared uneasily at the ship. 'Why don't they come out?'

'Maybe they've run into the power drain, just as we did,' suggested Jill. 'You remember, we could barely get our doors open.'

Peter cupped his hands. 'Come out whoever you are,' he shouted. 'The welcome party's here!'

As if in response there was a laboured hiss of hydraulic power. Slowly, very slowly, a landing ramp slid out of the ship and a door above it opened. Two squat metallic shapes glided swiftly down the ramp. Two more appeared in the doorway of the ship.

Jill Tarrant gave a gasp of horror. 'Daleks!'

One of the Daleks in the ship's doorway spoke in the metallic grating voice that the Doctor had known and hated for so long.

'The humans are to be exterminated. Fire at my command!'

The Daleks at the foot of the ramp swung their gun-sticks to cover the little party.

Railton ran forward, his arms held out in appeal. 'Wait a minute,' he called. 'Wait, please! You can't . . .'

The Dalek leader grated, '*Fire!*'

5

A Truce with Terror

Nothing happened.

The Dalek weapons gave a series of metallic clicks. 'Maximum power,' screamed the leader. 'Fire! Fire! Fire!'

There were more clicks. One of the Daleks swung its eye-stalk round towards its leader. 'Weaponry malfunction. Total power failure in all armament circuits.'

The stunned silence was broken by the sound of the Doctor's laughter. 'Well, well, well! Daleks—without the power to kill. How does it feel?'

He strolled closer to the ramp and the Dalek sentries swung their guns to cover him, emitting a further series of futile clicks. 'Keep back! Keep back!' There was a note of panic in the metallic screech.

The Doctor smiled. 'And if I don't, what will you do? Your weapons are useless here. They've been affected by the energy blackout that stranded the rest of us.'

The Dalek leader said arrogantly, 'The failure is temporary. Superior Dalek technology will overcome this interference. You will obey our orders.'

'You're not in any position to give orders,' pointed out the Doctor. 'We're all in this together. All equal—and all equally powerless.'

The Dalek responded to this taunt with one of the ranting, boasting speeches so common to its species.

'The Daleks are the supreme beings of the universe. Dalek technology is the most advanced in the entire cosmos.'

By now Railton had realised that his enemies really were helpless. 'Spare us the Dalek propaganda,' he said boldly. 'You're no better off than we are. What we ought to do is join forces.'

Rejection was automatic.

'The Daleks do not require the co-operation of inferior species.'

'Think about it,' urged Railton. 'There are five of us and only four of you. This planet is swarming with hostile aliens who want nothing better than to destroy all of us. Surely the fact must penetrate even Dalek arrogance!'

There was a brief silence. Then the Dalek leader said, 'We will confer.' The Daleks in the doorway disappeared into the ship. The two sentry Daleks glided up the ramp and followed them.

Railton mopped the sweat from his brow. 'Well, what do you think, Doctor?'

The Doctor said nothing for a moment. Railton's initiative in suggesting an alliance had taken him by surprise, and now he was busy thinking out possible moves and counter moves. 'It's a daring plan,' he said slowly. 'And they might just possibly agree with it. But I advise you not to trust them.'

'I don't,' said Railton grimly. 'But at the moment we need all the help we can get.'

'We don't need the Daleks,' said Galloway furiously. 'There's nothing they can do we can't do better on our own.'

'They happen to be brilliant technicians,' said the

Doctor quietly. 'Their inventive genius has made them one of the great powers of the universe. Bear that in mind.'

'Exactly,' agreed Railton. 'If they can find some way out of this, we can turn it to our advantage.'

Peter said miserably, 'But *Daleks*, sir! My father was killed in the Dalek wars. Dan lost his entire family. I hate the idea of co-operating with them.'

'Your father was just one man,' said Railton quietly. 'Millions will die if we can't get the Parrinium off of this planet.' He turned to the Doctor. 'Do you think they'll agree?'

The Doctor kept his eyes on the space ship door. 'I'm not sure. We'll just have to wait and see.'

The Dalek leader appeared in the doorway of the ship. 'We wish to confer further. You will be the spokesman. Come!' Its useless gun-stick was pointing at the Doctor. The Doctor hesitated, then shrugged. After all, they couldn't really harm him. Reflecting that it was a new sensation to enter a Dalek ship of his own accord, he climbed slowly up the ramp.

Time went by. The others waited, wondering what was going on inside that gleaming metal sphere. Peter drew Galloway aside. 'What do you think about this idea of co-operating with the Daleks?'

'It might work—for a while.'

'I think Railton's gone soft,' whispered Hamilton.

'Aye, mebbe so. He's scared of the wee salt-shakers, I can tell you that. I saw his face when they came out of the ship.'

'Look, our spokesman's coming back.'

The Doctor came back down the ramp.

'Well?' demanded Railton. 'What did they say?'

The Doctor rubbed his chin. 'They're still very suspicious, but I think they'll go along with your plan. They don't have much choice.' The Doctor's voice hardened. 'But I warn you, we must watch them all the time. We can't trust them an inch.'

'Did you manage to find out what they're doing here?' asked Jill.

'Several of their own colony planets are suffering from the disease. It seems even Daleks aren't immune. They need the Parrinium just as much as you do. That's why they may be prepared to co-operate.'

Inside the control room of the Dalek ship, a final conference was ending. 'It is agreed,' grated the Dalek leader. 'We will co-operate until the humans are of no further use to us. Our true motives in seeking the Parrinium must remain a secret. Understood. The humans must continue to believe that there are only four of us.' The Dalek leader swivelled its arm-stick towards the three other Daleks, unseen, and so far unsuspected, by the Doctor and his party. 'You will remain on board ship and carry out weaponry experiments as ordered.'

'We obey.'

The three Daleks glided away, and the other four moved towards the door.

The members of the Earth expedition waited tensely as four Daleks glided down the ramp towards them. Only the Doctor seemed calm.

'Well? Have you decided?'

'For the moment a truce exists between our party and yours.'

'Very well. It seems you're being sensible for once.' The Doctor sounded rather surprised.

'The truce will end when power is restored.'

'Agreed,' said Railton impatiently. 'Now, I suggest we all go over to our mining dome. We've located rich Parrinium deposits nearby and set up a dome to refine the ore. It's slow work without power though. Perhaps you can suggest some improvements in the technique.'

For a moment the Dalek leader made no reply. The Doctor guessed it was hard for a Dalek to accept orders, or even suggestions, from what it had been conditioned to regard as a member of an inferior species. Then it said, 'Very well. Lead the way. Lead!'

Trust a Dalek to make even an agreement sound like an order, thought the Doctor. He followed Railton and the others towards the dunes, uneasily conscious of the Daleks close behind him.

They had left the plain and were moving through a narrow canyon in the range of rocky hills when an arrow sped out of nowhere and buried itself in Railton's heart. He stared down at it in unbelieving astonishment, and fell dead to the ground.

The Doctor yelled, 'Get under cover!' and leaped for the shelter of a nearby boulder, waving to the others to do the same. He scanned the surrounding terrain. He saw only the high walls of the canyon, a scattering of boulders on the rocky hillside, the rounded shapes of the distant dunes. No movement, no sign of life.

Suddenly he realised Jill Tarrant was kneeling beside Railton's body, making a futile attempt to pull it under cover. 'Help me with him,' she sobbed. 'Doctor, help me.'

The Doctor ran to her side. 'Jill, leave him, he's dead. We can't help him now.'

Jill tugged at Railton's body. 'We can't just leave him here.'

A crude, stone-headed arrow struck the ground between them. The Doctor grabbed Jill's arm and yanked her back under cover.

Galloway wriggled close to him and pointed. 'The arrows came from over that way, behind those rocks.'

'Did you see anything?'

Galloway shook his head. A second shower of arrows whizzed towards them, thudding into the ground, and clattering against the rocks.

The Doctor said, 'It seems to be a fairly small group. If we break away and scatter we might stand a chance.'

'Just a minute, Doctor,' hissed Galloway furiously. 'I'm next in seniority to Railton. That puts me in command.'

The Doctor looked unbelievingly at him, astonished, not for the first time, at the rigidity of the military mind.

There was hysteria in Jill Tarrant's voice. 'All right, Commander. Give an order to get us out of this!'

Galloway glared furiously at her. He was about to make some angry reply when Peter Hamilton said, 'If you lot have finished arguing amongst yourselves—take a look around!'

They looked. A line of Exxilons had appeared on the skyline ahead of them. 'There are more over there,' said Hamilton. '*And* over there!'

There were Exxilons to their left and to their right, still more blocking the gully behind them. They were armed with a variety of primitive weapons—bows, spears, clubs, stone-headed axes. Stone age weapons, thought the Doctor, but on this planet they were the only ones that counted.

Galloway's hand was gripping the useless blaster at his belt. 'They're like sitting ducks. If only the guns were working.' Almost berserk with rage, he snatched the bow from his shoulder, fitted an arrow and fired. Clutching its chest, an Exxilon tumbled from a nearby boulder with a shrill cry of agony.

The Doctor ducked down, expecting a hail of arrows in reply. Instead there was a sudden flurry of movement amongst the Exxilons just ahead of them. Someone was being shoved to the front of the little group. 'Look,' gasped Jill. 'They've got Commander Stewart.'

The wounded man was being supported between two Exxilons. He was barely conscious, his head lolling on his chest. A third Exxilon menaced the wounded man's throat with a jagged stone knife. The message was clear.

Peter Hamilton said quietly. 'That settles it for me. We'll have to surrender. Jill?'

Her eyes fixed on the Commander, Jill nodded.

'What about you, Doctor?'

'I suppose so. When the only alternative to living is dying . . . What about our Dalek friends?'

All this time the little group of Daleks had taken no part in the action. Peter turned to them and called, 'We're going to surrender. What about you?'

The nearest Dalek trundled menacingly towards the Exxilons, acting from instinct rather than reason.

'Daleks do not surrender. Exterminate! Exterminate!'
A frantic clicking came from its useless weapon.

Immediately a shower of arrows rattled against its metal casing. There was triumph in the metallic voice. 'Primitive weaponry ineffective against superior Dalek shielding!'

A grinding sound came from above. A heavy boulder rolled down the hillside, smashing into the Dalek and knocking it on to its side. A swarm of Exxilons descended upon the disabled Dalek, bashing at it with clubs, axes and heavy rocks, hammering it into a shapeless lump of metal. The tremendous battering triggered the Dalek's self-destruct unit. Suddenly it exploded in smoke and flame, killing the nearest Exxilons and blowing several others off their feet. The survivors danced exultantly round the smoking pile of metal, screeching in triumph.

The Doctor looked at the remaining Daleks. 'You'll have to do better than that, won't you? What do you say now?'

The Dalek leader said tonelessly, 'We will appear to surrender. It will enable us to observe the enemy more closely.'

'That's a good face saving attitude. Well, let's get it over with!' The Doctor stepped out of cover, his hands held high, and the others followed.

The Exxilons closed in on them.

6

The Sacrifice

Somewhat to her own astonishment, Sarah was still alive. When she had been dragged to the altar, she had assumed that her end was literally minutes away. Presumably the high priest would produce his stone-bladed knife and that would be that.

In fact, things had gone rather differently. She had been lashed down upon the altar, held motionless by ropes at arms and wrists while around her the ceremony had gone on—and on and on.

There had been much chanting from the high priest, followed by responses from the crowd. Other priests had appeared to join in the ceremony. She had been sprinkled with strange fluids, menaced with various weapons, endlessly harangued by the priests. Incense-burners had been swung about her head; their thick, sweet-smelling smoke drifted across her face, almost choking her. Still the endless chanting and counter-chanting continued.

It was a funny thing to say about your own sacrifice, thought Sarah, but she was beginning to get rather bored with it all. To make things worse, the incense was making her dizzy. Suddenly the chanting rose to a crescendo and stopped. There was a moment of utter silence. The high priest loomed over her, and Sarah thought muzzily that surely this must be it. Curiously enough she felt no sensation of fear, just a calm acceptance.

But still there was no sign of the sacrificial knife. Instead the ropes were loosened and she was lifted from the altar. Her feet floated from under her, and without the support of the Exxilon priests she would have fallen. They began walking her towards the back of the cavern.

Sarah went meekly along with them. She seemed to have no will of her own and in some corner of her mind she realised that the smoke of the incense must contain a narcotic drug. But it didn't matter. All she had to do was walk, and everything would be all right . . .

The crowd drew back to form an alleyway, and Sarah walked between the two priests straight towards the black mouth of the tunnel.

At this moment the Doctor and his fellow prisoners were herded into the great cavern. It was obvious what was going on—the whole place reeked of ceremonial sacrifice.

The Doctor broke free from his Exxilon guards and ran the length of the great cavern before anyone could prevent him. 'Stop!' he shouted. 'Where are you taking her?' Grabbing the astonished high priest, and throwing him aside, he barged his way to Sarah's side, shoving the supporting priest away. 'Sarah, are you all right?'

Sarah stared dazedly up at him. She wanted to explain that he really mustn't interrupt the ceremony like this—but suddenly blackness closed in on her, and she slumped unconscious at his feet.

As the Doctor knelt to examine her the high priest barked a single guttural command and the two Exxilon priests descended on the Doctor, dragging him away.

Angrily he threw them aside again, fighting to get back to Sarah, but more and more Exxilons joined in the attack. They swarmed over the Doctor like huge black ants and he went down beneath the sheer weight of their attacking bodies. A stone club struck him a glancing blow on the head and he fell back unconscious.

Sarah woke up in a cage. 'First a church, now a zoo,' she thought. It was a very large cage, formed by setting bars across an alcove in the rock, and there were several other people in it with her. Muzzily, Sarah studied them. There was a heavily bandaged man lying unconscious in a corner. There were two other men, one young and brown-haired, one black-haired and burly, talking in low voices. On the far side of the cage, three squat metallic shapes were huddled in a group. Finally, to Sarah's immense relief, there was the Doctor, lying against the cavern wall not far away, with a fair-haired girl of about her own age examining a bruise on his forehead.

Slowly and carefully Sarah got up. She still felt weak at the knees, but her head was clear again. She went over to the girl and knelt beside her. 'Is the Doctor all right?'

'I think so. He seems to be coming round.'

Sarah rubbed her hand across her eyes. 'What happened?'

'Don't you remember?'

'It's all a bit hazy. They made me inhale some kind of drug.'

'Well, as far as I can gather, they were going to sacrifice you. Then we turned up, and the Doctor broke up the ceremony. He laid hands on their high priest—apparently that's about the worst crime you can commit on this planet. I'm afraid you two aren't very popular with our hosts!'

Sarah looked round the crowded cell. 'Who are you all? What are you doing here?'

The girl smiled wearily. 'That's a very long story. For a start, my name's Jill Tarrant . . .'

Peter Hamilton looked across the cage. The Doctor had recovered consciousness and was talking quietly to the two girls. Dan Galloway nodded towards him and said angrily, 'The man's crazy, I tell you. He's stirred them all up against us, ruined any chance we had of making a deal.'

'Come on, Dan,' said Peter quietly. 'He hadn't any choice. A couple of minutes more and that girl would probably have been dead.'

'So what? She's no concern of ours.'

Hamilton said, 'We're all in this together. It could have been me or you about to be sacrificed. Would you expect everybody else to stand by and let it happen?'

'The point is, it wasn't one of us. We've no loyalties to those two—they're simply not part of our mission.'

'So you'd let them die, just like that?'

Galloway leaned forward. 'You're forgetting something, Peter. Our job is to get hold of the Parrinium that will save the lives of millions. If a couple of people we don't even know have to die in the process—well, that's just too bad.'

The Daleks too had been conferring, and now their leader glided across to the two men. 'We have decided

53

the action we shall take. We will offer the Exxilons our knowledge and technology in return for their assistance. You would do well to do the same.'

Galloway grunted. 'Aye, well, anything's worth a try. Until we track down the cause of that power block, we'll none of us get off this planet.'

Hamilton nodded towards the Doctor and Sarah. 'What about them? Do you think the Exxilons will agree to let them go? I mean, we'll have to make that part of the deal . . .'

The eye-stalk of the Dalek leader swung round in his direction. 'The Doctor is an enemy of the Daleks. The girl is of no concern to us.'

Galloway said calmly. 'It seems we're in agreement about some things after all . . .'

The Doctor had made his usual amazingly rapid recovery, and was cheerfully lecturing the two girls on the nature of primitive societies. 'The more primitive the society, the more complex the taboos. The sacrifice has to be made in exactly the right way, all the rituals observed, step by step. When I arrived and interrupted things, they had no alternative but to stop the ceremony.'

'So what do you think will happen now?' asked Sarah.

'I'm afraid that what they had planned for you has merely been postponed. And there'll probably be two of us starring in the next performance.'

Sarah tried to smile. 'Well, it's always nice to have company. Jill, what's the matter?'

Jill was staring across the cage. 'Galloway seems to be getting very thick with the Daleks. I don't know what he's up to, but I don't like the look of it.'

54

Galloway and the Dalek leader had gone to the bars of the cage and seemed to be trying to communicate with an Exxilon priest outside.

The Doctor said quietly. 'I have a feeling it might be better if you didn't involve yourself with us, Miss Tarrant. We seem to be the flies in a very nasty jar of ointment.'

After much guttural muttering from the Exxilons, a door in the bars had been opened, and Galloway and the Dalek leader were allowed to pass through. Jill gave the Doctor a worried look. 'I imagine they're trying to negotiate some kind of deal—a way for all of us to get out of here.'

'All of us?' The Doctor shook his head. 'That's wishful thinking, my dear. The Daleks certainly won't do anything to help me. And I don't expect too much from your friend Galloway either.'

In the small, compact laboratory of the Dalek space ship an experiment was in progress. There had been a significant modification in the appearance of the three Daleks left inside the ship. Instead of the now-useless blasters, another kind of weapon had been fitted to the squat metallic bodies. It consisted of a simple gun-barrel with an ammunition magazine clipped underneath.

On a bench at the other end of the laboratory was a target—a miniature TARDIS. One of the Daleks moved to the firing position. There was a staccato chattering sound and smoke drifted from its gun muzzle. The model TARDIS disintegrated in a shower of plastic fragments.

The Dalek glided to the bench. 'Target model completely destroyed. Substitute weaponry now functioning satisfactorily.'

'We will proceed immediately with the second stage of our plan.'

The three Daleks glided from the laboratory, and along the short metal corridor that led to the exit ramp. Soon they were moving along the path followed by the prisoners some time earlier.

Two Exxilons appeared on the rocks above them, both armed with bows. They fired and the stone-headed arrows bounced harmlessly from the Daleks' metal casing. Immediately the leading Dalek swivelled round, aiming its gun. There was a rattle of machine-gun fire and the Exxilons were blasted from the rocks by the impact of the heavy bullets. They crashed down on to the stony ground behind the path, lying like two bundles of black rags.

Impassively, the leading Dalek said, 'Modified weapons moderately efficient when tested in action.'

The Daleks glided along the path. Behind them the blood of the Exxilons soaked into the rocky ground.

The gate in the bars opened. Galloway and the Dalek leader entered, the Exxilon high priest behind them. More Exxilon priests followed them into the cell. The high priest pointed to the Doctor and Sarah. The priests caught hold of them and began pulling them from the cell. Jill Tarrant cried, 'No!' and tried to stop them. A savage shove from one of the Exxilons sent her reeling away.

Hamilton turned to Galloway as the Doctor and Sarah were dragged out. 'Dan, we've got to do something.'

Galloway shook his head. 'Don't interfere. We've got to think of ourselves now, and what we came here to do.'

Hamilton grabbed him by the arm. 'What happened out there, Dan? What did you agree to?'

Galloway pulled away. 'We managed to communicate with the Exxilons. They speak a kind of pigeon galactic, though it's so debased you can hardly follow them. We made a deal—at least, the Dalek did. The Exxilons seem impressed by that armour of theirs.'

'A deal that includes the sacrifice of the Doctor and Sarah, I suppose? And you agreed?'

Galloway turned away. 'There was nothing else I could do.'

The Dalek leader moved across to them. 'Exxilons refuse to discuss final terms until interrupted sacrifices have been completed. We will follow and observe.'

The Daleks glided from the cell, and Exxilon priests herded Jill and Hamilton after them. Galloway was about to follow when he heard a feeble voice calling his name. 'Galloway . . .'

He turned and saw Commander Stewart struggling to sit up. Galloway went to kneel beside him. The Commander's face was grey, and his breath came in rattling gasps. It was clear that rough handling on top of his other wounds had been too much for his weakened constitution. Commander Stewart was dying. Hoarsely he whispered, 'I heard everything. Galloway. You are not fit to command this expedition.'

Galloway met the dying man's eyes without flinching. 'I'm only doing what's necessary, sir. I'm going to get that Parrinium *whatever the cost.*'

'You're a glory hunter, Galloway,' said the feeble voice. 'You always were. I never trusted you. Now I'm giving my last order. I'm appointing Hamilton over you.'

The voice was almost inaudible. Galloway thrust his lips close to the Commander's ear. 'Sir, you can't do that. He's just not tough enough.'

'It's done,' whispered Stewart triumphantly. 'Peter Hamilton will take command. That is an order . . . an order . . .' Stewart's head fell back. A spasm of coughing shook the wounded body, and then he lay still.

Dan Galloway stared down at his Commander's body. They had never got on—not that Galloway got on with anyone very much. They had clashed over Galloway's ruthless methods on previous expeditions, and Galloway suspected that the Commander had blocked his overdue promotion.

Dan Galloway was essentially a simple man. He had lost all his family in one of the early Dalek wars, grown up as a ragged poverty-stricken refugee, joined the Marine Space Corps at the first opportunity, and clawed his way up from the ranks. Morals and ideals were the kind of luxuries he had never been able to afford. He had only one standard of behaviour—whatever helped Dan Galloway to succeed was justified. Even if it meant co-operation with the Daleks . . .

He wondered if Commander Stewart had been right about his motives. The man who brought this expedition to a successful conclusion would be a hero on a hundred planets, rich and famous for the rest of his life.

Why shouldn't he be that man? In any case motives were unimportant. Results were what counted. This expedition had to succeed. But not with Peter Hamilton in command. He was too soft—like Railton and Stewart before him.

The sound of chanting came from the cavern outside. The sacrifice was under way. Once the girl and the Doctor were dead, he would find some way of outwitting both Daleks and Exxilons, and getting the Parrinium away from the planet.

Galloway pulled the space-blanket over the dead man's face. 'I'm sorry, Commander,' he said quietly. 'I didn't quite catch what you said.'

He turned and went out of the cage.

7

Escape to the Unknown

Sarah felt trapped in a recurring nightmare. Once
again she stood before the altar, surrounded by black-
robed figures. Once again the air was filled with low,
chanting voices and the sweet sickly reek of the narcotic
incense. The only difference, though it was a consider-
able one, was the fact that now the Doctor was at her
side.

They had reached the point at which the Doctor had
interrupted the earlier ceremony. Sarah glanced up at
him and gave a slight jerk of her head. Should they
make a run for it? The Doctor shook his head, and
Sarah saw his lips form the words, 'Not yet.' No doubt
the Doctor had some brilliant plan . . .

In fact the Doctor had no plan at all, though he was
desperately trying to think of one. His only thought was
that it would be better to let the ceremony get well
under way before making any move. He was confident
that he could resist the drugged incense smoke, and
there was a chance that the Exxilons, half hypnotised
by their own ritual, might react too slowly to prevent
their getaway. What he desperately needed now was a
diversion.

Jill Tarrant and Peter Hamilton watched in unbelieving horror. Hamilton was in an agony of inde-
cision. He felt he couldn't stand by and see two people

sacrificed—yet there was nothing he could do to help. He glanced at Dan Galloway who stood watching the ceremony, his heavy features impassive. Behind him were the three Daleks.

In the corner of his eye Hamilton saw movement at the cave mouth, and turned to look behind him. To his astonishment three more Daleks were standing there. There was something different about them, about their weapons . . . Some instinct made him yell, 'Look out!' and shove Jill and Galloway to one side.

The cavern echoed with the roar of the Dalek machine-guns. The three Daleks fired ruthlessly into the packed crowd and all around Exxilons were smashed to the ground by the impact of the heavy bullets. They milled round frantically in a useless attempt to escape, and the Daleks mowed them down in rows. The air was filled with the harsh chatter of the guns and the screams of the dying.

Even though the Doctor and Sarah were some way from the re-armed Daleks, bullets were whistling around them. The Exxilon priest at Sarah's side staggered and fell, blood spreading over the front of his ceremonial robes. The Doctor grabbed Sarah's hand and dragged her behind the altar. He looked round for a way of escape. There was only one.

Holding Sarah by the hand he pulled her across the cavern, past the bodies of dead and wounded Exxilons, and into the mouth of the tunnel.

They ran on into the darkness until the sounds of slaughter faded away behind them. Sarah stumbled, and fell, feeling suddenly exhausted. She lay gasping for a moment, and the Doctor helped her to sit up. 'Just rest for a moment. The Daleks don't seem to be following us, and the Exxilons have got other things to worry about.'

'Those Dalek things,' gasped Sarah. 'Where did they come from? They're not locals, are they?'

'No, indeed. The Daleks originated on the planet Skaro. They're probably the most technically advanced and utterly ruthless life-form in the galaxy—a fact you've just seen demonstrated. The Daleks are old enemies of mine.'

'If they're robots, why isn't their power affected? How come they can still move?'

'Probably because they're not really robots at all. Inside each of those metal shells is a living, bubbling lump of hate!' The Doctor helped Sarah to her feet. 'Come on, we'd better be on our way.'

They moved off down the tunnel.

Those Exxilons who were still left alive clustered together in a terrified group, covered by two of the newly armed Daleks. The other Dalek reported to the leader. 'All resistance has ceased.'

'I will speak to the high priest. Bring him to me.' As the Dalek moved away, Galloway came forward. 'What are you going to talk to him about?'

'We still require the co-operation of the Exxilons. Now they will co-operate on our terms.'

'What will you do if they don't agree?'

'We shall select groups of hostages for extermination until they obey.'

Galloway nodded, quite unmoved. 'That should bring them round to our way of thinking. The first thing to do is make them supply working parties to mine the Parrinium. Then we must start tackling that power block—'

'Silence. Your advice is not required.'

'Now wait a minute,' began Galloway angrily. 'We agreed to work together . . .'

'The Daleks are in command. You will obey.'

Galloway took an angry step forward and one of the Daleks guarding the Exxilons swung its machine-gun to cover him. He bowed his head. 'All right, all right. Whatever you say . . .'

The tunnel wound on and on and Sarah began to wonder if it went clear to the centre of the planet. Luckily they weren't in complete darkness. Here and there glowing crystals set into the rocky walls gave a kind of subdued glow. As they trudged along Sarah looked up at the Doctor, who seemed lost in thought.

'Doctor?'

'What is it?'

'You remember all that mumbo-jumbo back there— it *was* a sacrificial ceremony of some kind, wasn't it?'

'That seemed to be the general idea.'

'Well, as far as I can remember, the high point of the ceremony was going to be when I was sent off down this tunnel.'

'That's right.'

'Well, how were they sacrificing me by just dumping me down here?'

'Ah! I was afraid you'd think of that sooner or later.'

'Well?'

'Well, what?' said the Doctor evasively.

'You do have an idea—about what they were up to?'

63

'Yes, but it isn't one of my favourites. In fact I don't much care for it at all.'

'Come on, Doctor. You might as well share it.'

'If you insist. I think the Exxilons expected the sacrifice to be completed for them—by something that lives in the tunnel.'

'Sort of like throwing us to the sacred crocodiles?'

'That's right. I could be wrong of course . . .'

An ear-splitting howl echoed down the tunnel from somewhere ahead of them.

Sarah shivered. 'Doctor—next time you get an idea—just keep it to yourself, will you?'

Ignored and apparently forgotten, Jill Tarrant and Peter Hamilton waited in a quiet corner of the cavern, wondering what was going on. Leaving the three armed Daleks in charge, the three rescued Daleks had left, presumably to go back to their ship. Shortly afterwards they had returned, and now they too were fitted with machine-guns.

The Dalek leader was dictating his terms to the high priest. Dan Galloway hovered on the fringe of the group, not daring to speak, but desperate to keep some vestige of his status as a Dalek ally.

The Daleks and Exxilons moved away, and Galloway came over to rejoin the others.

Jill looked at him. 'Well? What are your new friends up to now?'

'Oh, it's all agreed. We've finalised a deal with the Exxilons.'

Hamilton laughed scornfully. 'We?'

Galloway's face darkened with anger. 'The Exxilons

will provide a work force to help mine the Parrinium. We'll be in charge of that, together with some of the Daleks.'

'What about the rest of them?'

'They're sending a patrol to the City to investigate the cause of the power block.'

'And what are the Exxilons getting out of this deal?'

'Oh, nothing much.'

'Tell us,' insisted Jill.

'Well, it appears the Exxilons have some kind of enemy—a sort of breakaway group of their own people. We've agreed to help the Exxilons wipe them out.'

'You've agreed to *what*?'

'In return the Exxilons guarantee us all the Parrinium we need. We'll save the lives of millions . . .'

'And how many will you murder to do it?' asked Jill furiously. 'You *can't* accept terms like that!'

'They're only Exxilons, primitives,' said Galloway calmly. 'They don't count.' He hesitated. 'There's one more thing . . .'

'All right,' said Hamilton grimly. 'Tell us the rest of it. What else have you agreed?'

Galloway looked shamefaced. 'This is the bit you won't like. That fellow they call the Doctor . . . The Exxilons want him punished, and so do the Daleks. He's to be found and brought back—dead or alive.'

Hamilton said wearily, 'You're totally ruthless, aren't you, Galloway? So now the Daleks are hunting the Doctor too?'

Galloway nodded. 'A couple of them have gone down the tunnel after him—just in case whatever lives down there doesn't get him first.'

*

The Doctor and Sarah moved cautiously onwards. The Doctor noticed an increasing number of fissures appearing the rock walls, but they all seemed too narrow to offer any chance of escape. Another of the mysterious howls echoed down the tunnel. Sarah looked uneasily at the Doctor. 'That sounded awfully close.'

'Oh, just some sort of subterranean wind effect, I imagine.'

'Who are you trying to kid?'

'Myself, chiefly!' admitted the Doctor.

There was another roar, louder this time.

Further back down the tunnel, the pursuing Daleks heard the sound. They paused for a moment, then glided swiftly onwards.

The Doctor and Sarah came to another, deeper fissure in the rock wall on their left. The Doctor glanced cautiously at it as they went past. It was impossible to tell how deep it was, but the Doctor thought it was probably too narrow to conceal any life form. They hurried on their way.

The Doctor was wrong. As soon as he had moved past, a hand and a long thin arm appeared out of the crack. The hand was totally white, like that of some creature that never sees the light. The rest of the creature's body was grey and it oozed out of the crack like toothpaste from a tube. It padded softly down the tunnel after the Doctor and Sarah.

*

The tunnel began to widen, and rounding a bend they suddenly found themselves at a junction point. Here the tunnel suddenly divided itself in three. They could carry on straight ahead, they could follow the tunnel on the left, or they could turn down the equally large tunnel on the right.

It was like some old fable, thought Sarah. Three choices to make. Suppose only one of the tunnels led to safety, and the other two meant death? How were they going to choose? With three choices you couldn't even spin a coin.

The weird howling filled the air again. By some freak of the tunnel's acoustics it seemed to come from all around them. It was impossible to tell from which of the three tunnels it was coming.

'I can hear your wind effect gnashing its teeth, Doctor,' said Sarah nervously.

'Pure imagination—I hope!' The Doctor listened keenly as the uncanny sound came again. 'There's something funny about that noise. It sounds mechanical, or electronic. Not like an animal sound at all.'

'That's a great consolation. Well, which way do we go?'

The Doctor indicated the left hand tunnel. 'I think I'll make a little reconnaissance down this one.'

'Right!' Sarah moved forward.

'Alone, Sarah.'

'Alone?'

'I don't want anything coming down that tunnel behind me to cut off my retreat. With you on watch here, you can give me a warning.'

'And who's going to warn me?' asked Sarah indignantly.

67

The Doctor grinned. 'Oh, you're in a good safe position. After all, you've got three different ways to run!' He paused at the left-hand opening. 'I'll try it for about half a mile. If things look promising, I'll come back to fetch you.'

'And if they don't?'

'I'll come back even quicker, and we'll try another tunnel.' With a nod of farewell, the Doctor disappeared, and Sarah was left alone.

Or was she? She seemed to hear the faintest of sounds—a soft, almost inaudible padding. Sarah whirled round and listened. For a moment there was only silence, then she heard the sound again. Something was creeping along the main tunnel towards her.

She peered into the semi-darkness, but there was nothing to be seen. 'Anybody there?' she called. There was no reply.

Suddenly the weird howling sound rang out again. Caught between two terrors, Sarah turned. Had the Doctor chosen the wrong tunnel and run straight into the monster? The howl died away. The silence returned and Sarah heard that faint padding sound again. She looked over her shoulder—and jumped with horror. A ghostly grey figure was standing in the tunnel behind her.

The Doctor had just reached a sharp turning in the tunnel, when the howl came again, louder this time. Whatever was making it was very close. Clearly he'd chosen the wrong tunnel after all. The Doctor knew he ought to turn back for Sarah, but curiosity drove him on. At least he could get a look at the thing before he retreated. He rounded the bend—and found himself facing an enormous silvery snake. It was rearing up so that its blunt head hung in mid-air high above him. Its one eye glowing a fiery red, the giant creature loomed over him. The great, flat head weaved to and fro as if searching for prey.

8

Bellal

The Doctor backed slowly away.

The silver snake reared higher, weaving its head to and fro as if searching for him. It gave a weird electronic howl. The blunt head stabbed suddenly towards him, and now the Doctor saw that it wasn't a living creature at all. It was made of flexible metallic tubing, and the red eye was a monitor lens. The length of the thing was enormous. It stretched back and back, until it disappeared into the darkness of the tunnel.

Not a snake then, decided the Doctor, but part of a mechanised root system—a kind of extendable probe, presumably sent out by the City. In that case why the howl? To scare off intruders? Or perhaps the noise acted as a kind of sonar, detecting the presence of intruders by bouncing off sound waves . . . The Doctor received sudden, unwelcome confirmation of his theory. The probe howled again, then, as if the sound had given it a fix, it slithered suddenly towards him.

The Doctor backed away, and tripped over a loose chunk of rock. The fall saved his life. The probe lunged with the speed of a striking cobra, and a bolt of energy sizzled over the Doctor's head, blasting a chunk out of the tunnel wall. The Doctor rolled over, sprang to his feet, and ran. The probe undulated after him, making a hungry, moaning sound.

The Doctor shot back round the bend, spotted another rock-fissure on his right and squeezed himself into it. He wriggled back and back into the darkness until the fissure became too narrow for him to go further. He saw the gleaming metal probe shoot past the fissure. It howled again, then stopped and hovered, realising that somehow it had lost its prey. Red eye glowing in the darkness, the blunt head hovered in mid-air, hunting for the Doctor . . .

Sarah gazed at the ghastly apparition in horror. It took a pace forward, and Sarah backed hurriedly away. 'Keep back! Keep away from me . . .'

The apparition spoke. 'Please . . . do not be afraid.' Its voice was low and gentle, almost child-like.

As she began to recover from the shock of its sudden appearance, Sarah realised the creature wasn't so very terrifying after all. To begin with it was very small, not much bigger than a child. It wore a tattered greenish garment that covered arms and legs and body so closely that at first sight it looked like the creature's skin. The head was small and round, completely hairless, with small ears and enormous staring eyes. The face was a dull, fish-belly white, and seemed to be faintly luminous. With a sudden lizard-like movement, the creature scuttled closer. 'I mean you no harm. I will help you if I can.'

'Who are you?' whispered Sarah.

'I am called Bellal. I am an Exxilon, a native of this planet. But my people do not share the beliefs of those others, the ones who tried to sacrifice you. They consider us their enemies.'

Sarah thought it was bad enough being on this planet, without having to listen to a lecture on its politics. But there was something curiously appealing about the white-faced little creature, and it seemed anxious to enlighten her. 'And are you?' she asked. 'Are you their enemies?'

Bellal shook his head. 'We seek only to save the entire Exxilon race from destruction. But we do not share their beliefs, or worship the City as they do, and for that we are persecuted and driven to live in secret, deep beneath the planet. We are the Subterranean Exxilons.'

'How many of you are there?'

'We are very few—few, against so many enemies. Please, I will answer all your questions, but it is too dangerous here. Let me take you to a place of safety.'

'I'm sorry, but I can't leave here. I must wait for—'

'You have a companion? Which way did he go?'

Sarah pointed to the left hand tunnel. 'Down there.'

Bellal gave a little hiss of alarm. 'That way lies death.'

'Then we must find the Doctor and warn him. Please, come with me.'

Bellal said reluctantly. 'It may already be too late. But I will do what I can.'

Another little creature scuttled out of the darkness, so like Bellal as to be almost identical. 'The machine-creatures from the space ship . . . Two of them . . . they are very close.'

'Machine creatures?' said Sarah. 'You mean Daleks?'

Bellal grasped Sarah's arm and pulled her into a nearby fissure. He and his companion crowded in behind her, shielding her with their bodies. Sarah realised that their greyish garments blended perfectly with the walls of the tunnel, forming a perfect camouflage.

Two Daleks glided into view. They drew to a halt at the sight of the three entrances facing them. They hovered for a moment, eye-sticks swivelling uneasily to and fro. Then the one in the lead said, 'We will search independently. Fugitives are to be exterminated on sight.'

'I obey.' The harsh metallic voices echoed through the tunnels. The Daleks separated and moved off, one to the left and one to the right.

As soon as they were out of sight Sarah wriggled out of her hiding-place. 'One of those Daleks will be coming up behind the Doctor. We must go and warn him.'

Bellal gripped her arm, holding her back. 'It will be of no use. You must stay silent, or we will all be killed. You must understand . . . It is beyond anyone's power to help your companion now.'

The Doctor was reaching a similar conclusion. In his desperate dash for safety he had run straight into a trap. He couldn't go on because the crack became too narrow. He couldn't go back because the probe was still hovering outside the fissure, trying to work out what had happened to its prey. The Doctor had hoped that it would eventually give up and go away, but he had underestimated its persistence.

It was only a servo-mechanism of limited intelligence, he thought. But it was obviously programmed to seek out and destroy intruders, and not to give up until it had found them. It wouldn't take even the dimmest mechanical mind much longer to work out that there was only one place the Doctor could be. And once it had him located, it need only blast a few energy-bolts down the fissure and that would be that. It was a wonder it hadn't found him already. Perhaps the narrowness of the rock-fissure was confusing its sonar.

Suddenly the probe appeared, directly outside the fissure. The red eye-lens glowed, as it moved cautiously towards the crack. Surely it would spot him any moment now . . .

Help came at last, not from the Doctor's friends, but from his greatest enemies. A Dalek appeared down the tunnel, and the probe withdrew from the crack, and whipped round to face this new threat.

From his hiding place inside the crack the Doctor had a grandstand view of the confrontation. The Dalek stopped short as the snake-like metal form of the probe hovered in the air above it. The probe hovered over the Dalek, its red eye seeming to blink in astonishment. For a moment the two metal monsters studied each other.

Then the Dalek made its predictable response to the unknown danger. With a harsh cry of 'Exterminate!' it opened fire on the probe. At exactly the same moment the probe made the same decision, and lunged forward, blasting the Dalek with an energy-bolt.

There was an explosive crackle of fierce blue sparks and the Dalek spun round, cannoning into the rock wall, like a demented dodgem-car. At the same time some of the Dalek's bullets struck the probe; it lashed about the tunnel in panic-stricken fury.

The Dalek swivelled round, trying to bring its machine-gun to bear. 'I am under attack,' it screeched. 'Assist! Assist! Assist!'

Before the Dalek could take aim the probe lunged

forward again, blasting the Dalek with another energy-bolt. The Dalek spun round, smashing into the rock wall. 'Oh good shot, sir!' called the Doctor delightedly. 'A hit, a palpable hit!' He moved to the end of the fissure to get a better view.

With an angry howl the probe reared to its full height. Then it lunged forward again and again, blasting the stricken Dalek with a rain of energy-bolts. The Dalek blew up.

Back at the junction point, Sarah was listening to the sounds of battle. They rose to a crescendo, there was the sound of a distant explosion—then silence.

Shaking off Bellal's restraining hand, Sarah headed determinedly for the left-hand tunnel. Bellal darted in front of her, barring her way. 'No!' he hissed.

'I must find out what's happening to the Doctor . . .'

'The other Dalek will come back this way,' said Bellal desperately. 'We must leave.'

'The Doctor may be hurt. I've got to find him.'

'As soon as it is safe, I will send some of our people to look for him,' promised Bellal. 'Now we must leave here . . .' He broke off. 'No . . . it is too late. There is something coming . . . Quick!' whispered Bellal. He dragged Sarah back to the fissure where they'd hidden before, and his companion ran to join them.

Tensely Sarah watched the tunnel entrance. The sound of movement came nearer, a shadow loomed up —and the muzzle of a Dalek machine-gun appeared . . .

Sarah shrank back—and the Doctor moved warily into view, holding the machine-gun before him.

With a sob of relief, she ran forwards, throwing herself

into his arms. 'Doctor, you're safe. What happened? How did you get away from the Dalek? What did you see down there?'

The Doctor grinned. 'Steady on, Sarah, one thing at a time. I had a confrontation with a rather nasty root—a kind of probe.'

'A root?'

'That's right. I think it was part of the City's defences.' The Doctor smiled. 'It wasn't very fond of me, but it positively hated the Dalek!'

'So what happened?'

'Probe City—one, Dalek United—nil,' said the Doctor happily. 'It blew the Dalek to bits.' He held up the machine-gun. 'I managed to salvage this from the wreckage—it was about the only bit left undamaged.' He tossed it aside.

Bellal and his companion came forward from the fissure, and the Doctor swung round. 'It's all right, Doctor, they're friends,' said Sarah. She gave the Doctor a brief account of her meeting with Bellal and his companion. 'They say they're part of a group who oppose the other Exxilons.'

'How do you do, gentlemen,' said the Doctor politely. 'We could certainly do with some allies.'

The little Exxilon gave a kind of bow. 'We shall try to help you, Doctor. My companion here is called Gotal—' Bellal broke off. He ran to the right-hand tunnel, and stood listening. 'I think I hear movement. The other Dalek must be coming.'

Gotal was hovering impatiently by the entrance to the central tunnel. 'This way. Come quickly!'

The Doctor and Sarah ran into the tunnel, and Bellal

followed. Soon all four had disappeared into the darkness.

A few minutes later the second Dalek came back down the right-hand tunnel. It turned towards the left-hand entrance then paused, seeming to sense some movement. It hovered for a moment—then set off after the Doctor and his companions.

9

The Pursuit

The little party hurried down the central tunnel, Gotal leading the way, followed by the Doctor and Sarah. Bellal himself brought up the rear, pausing from time to time to listen. The Doctor could hear nothing, but he imagined long residence underground had made Bellal's hearing particularly acute. Bellal hurried forward, urging them on. 'Move more quickly. The Dalek is coming this way, and it is gaining on us.'

They ran on down the tunnel at a terrible pace, until suddenly Gotal stopped. The way ahead was blocked by a fall of rock. 'It's a dead end,' said Sarah. 'We're trapped.'

Bellal was scanning the pile of rubble with an expert eye. 'Not quite. See! There at the top' He pointed, and they saw a little gap at the top of the pile of rubble.

The Doctor looked at the narrow space. 'Through there? I'll never make it!'

'It is the only way,' said Gotal. He began scrambling up the rock pile, with the others following.

Gotal slipped through the little gap with ease. He and his people were used to wriggling through cramped spaces underground. Even Sarah got through without much difficulty.

It was the Doctor who found himself in trouble.

Although he was thin, he was tall and broad shouldered as well, and he soon began to feel that squeezing himself through the narrow gap was next to impossible. With a desperate heave he wriggled half-way through the gap—and then stuck.

'Hurry, Doctor,' urged Bellal. 'The Dalek is very close now.'

The Doctor stretched an arm out in front of him. 'Sarah, give me a pull from your side will you?'

Sarah grasped the Doctor's wrist and pulled with all her might. Bellal put his shoulder against the Doctor and shoved with surprising strength. They all heaved—and the Doctor shot through the narrow space like a cork coming out of a bottle, just as the Dalek appeared behind them.

Baffled by the rock-pile, the Dalek halted—Daleks cannot climb. With an angry cry of 'Exterminate! Exterminate!' it sent a fusillade of bullets after the disappearing Bellal.

'Down!' yelled the Doctor. They all threw themselves down as Dalek bullets whistled over their heads. They howled and ricochetted down round the tunnel, bringing a shower of rock-chips down on their heads. The Doctor and his companions lay face down, like a patrol caught in no-man's-land. The roar of the firing ended at last, and there was silence. Either the Dalek had run out of ammunition, or it had become discouraged and gone away. Cautiously the Doctor raised his head. 'I think it's gone now. Everyone all right?'

He got to his feet, and the others did the same, dusting themselves down. 'We can rest for a while,' whispered Bellal. 'We are safe now—for a time.'

The Doctor stretched. 'Maybe so—but we can't just

stay hiding underground. We've got to get back power for the TARDIS, for one thing—and for another, we must do what we can to help the mission from Earth.'

Sarah was all in favour of getting away, but she didn't much fancy risking her life for people who'd abandoned them. 'They'll be all right, won't they? They seem to be pretty pally with the Daleks.'

The Doctor shook his head. 'There may be an alliance of some kind for the moment. But take it from me—the moment they cease to be useful, the Daleks will wipe them out without a qualm.' The Doctor shook his head worriedly. 'I only wish I knew what was going on up there.'

'One of my people is watching, Doctor,' said Bellal. 'He will report to me soon. Come, I will take you to our base.'

The Subterranean Exxilon was called Jebal, and he lay wrapped in his cloak at the top of a dune that over-looked the mining area. The coarse-woven garment was exactly the same colour as the sand, and Jebal's tiny form was almost invisible. Like most of his people Jebal hated being out in the open, especially during daylight. The burning sun scorched his delicate white skin, and its glare dazzled his sensitive eyes, which were adapted to the permanent semi-darkness of the caves. Shading them with his hand he peered over the edge of the dune, trying to work out what was going on below.

A little group of Exxilons was chipping at the rocky outcrop with simple store tools. Not Jebal's people, but the savage surface Exxilons. Standing over them were two aliens. One was human from the Earth expedition, the other one of the machine-creatures, the Daleks. They were engaged in angry discussion.

The Dalek scanned the working party with its eye-stick, then swivelled back towards Galloway. 'The Exxilons are working too slowly.'

'Aye, and I'm not surprised. With the kind of primitive equipment they use . . .' The use of any kind of modern equipment was apparently against the Exxilon religion. The power drills were useless anyway because of the energy-blockage, but the Exxilons refused even to use the picks and shovels the Earth expedition could supply. They were chipping at the Parrinium-bearing rock with a variety of stone-age tools, and not surprisingly the work went with infuriating slowness.

The Dalek knew all this, but it was concerned only with results. 'The workers must work more quickly, and the work force must be increased. You will arrange it.'

'You arrange it,' growled Galloway. 'That high priest isn't exactly co-operative, for all your threats. We were lucky to get this many workers.'

Faced with opposition, the Dalek simply repeated its command. 'More workers! More! Exxilons will obey our commands.'

'And if they don't?'

'They will be exterminated. Go and tell them.'

Galloway turned away muttering, 'I'm not running errands for you. We made an agreement. We're supposed to be allies.'

'It was expedient at the time. Now it is no longer necessary. You will live only as long as you serve the Daleks. You will obey!'

Galloway had no particular objection to bullying and threatening the Exxilons, particularly if it would get the work done quicker. But to act as an errand-boy for the Daleks offended his dignity. 'I won't do it, I tell you. Go yourself.'

The Dalek's machine-gun swung round to cover him. 'Obey the Daleks,' it grated. 'Obey! Obey!'

Galloway glared furiously at the metal shape before him. But he knew he was beaten. The Dalek would kill him without a second's hesitation if it decided he was no longer useful. 'All right, all right,' he muttered. He turned and headed in the direction of the great cavern.

In a little cave deep below the surface of the planet, the Doctor and Sarah were sharing a meal with Bellal and some of his people. It wasn't much of a meal—brackish water in a stone jug, some coarse black bread, and a few wizened fruits, but it was better than nothing, and the Doctor and Sarah ate hungrily. The little group of Subterraneans devoured the food with relish, and Sarah guessed that even this simple food was in short supply.

The cave had been turned into a simple communal dining and living area, with beds in niches around the walls, and roughly shaped stone chairs and tables. It was clear that for these Exxilons as for those on the surface, life was hard and primitive, a perpetual struggle for survival. Sarah finished the last of her fruit, and turned to Bellal. 'As far as I can gather, this City seems to be the cause of all the trouble. Where did it come from? Who built the wretched thing?'

Bellal said sadly, 'You do not know? But of course, how could you realise? We built the City ourselves, we Exxilons.'

Sarah looked round the cave, which bore all the signs of a culture not much above the stone age. She thought of the savage Exxilons of the surface, with their bows and arrows and ritual sacrifice. And she thought of the City, gleaming remote and beautiful, towering high above the stony desert. 'I'm sorry, I don't understand. How could you have ...' her voice tailed away in embarrassment.

Bellal was well aware what she was thinking. 'The Exxilons were not always savages.' His voice changed, becoming a sort of ritual chant as he recited the tragic history of his people. 'Exxilon had grown old before life had ever begun on Earth. Our ancestors solved the great mysteries of science. They built craft that travelled through space. They were the supreme beings of the galaxy.'

The Doctor was listening in fascination. 'What ended their power?' he asked gently. 'Was it war?' The Doctor knew of all too many planets where great scientific achievement had ended in mindless self-destruction.

Bellal shook his head. 'No. Yet it is true that our ancestors created their own destruction. They built the City.' Bellal paused, overcome by emotion. His voice steadied and he went on, 'They dreamed of crowning their civilisation with one supreme achievement. Using all their knowledge, all their energies, they planned to build the ultimate City, a City that would be greater than any in the cosmos—a City that would outlast Time itself.'

Sarah said, 'Well, it looks as if they succeeded. When I saw the place it looked as if it had been built only yesterday.'

Bellal went on, 'They used their scientific brilliance to make the City into a living being, an entity that could protect itself, repair itself, absorb the energy it needed directly from the air of the planet and turn it to any use. They even gave it a brain.'

'I see,' said the Doctor softly. 'So the City became a single living thing—greater and more powerful than the many who built it?'

Bellal nodded. 'By the time the City was completed, it realised that only one thing flawed its perfection—the Exxilons, the inferior beings who had created it. Our ancestors realised too late that they had created a monster. They tried to destroy the City—and it used the weapons they had given it to destroy them. It drove out the survivors, and barred its gates forever. Now we, and those others you met on the surface are all that remain. We have become savages.'

'You're not a savage, Bellal,' said Sarah. 'Though I can't say as much for the others. Why are you so different from them?'

'When the City expelled them, most of the Exxilon people turned against science and progress completely. Any culture, any invention, progress of any kind became completely forbidden. They rejected the City and all it stood for. They deliberately turned themselves into savages. But although they hate the City, they fear it too. Over the long years it became their god—a cruel and savage god. They worship it, and they make sacrifices to it.'

'Yes, I know,' said Sarah. 'We almost qualified for that ourselves.'

The Doctor said, 'But you Subterraneans don't worship the City?'

'We hate and fear it, but we do not worship it. The City absorbs all life, all energy from our planet, turning it into a desert. Constantly it rebuilds and improves itself, while outside its walls we, the Exxilons, starve and die. Every year the food grows less, and our numbers grow fewer. Our aim is to destroy the City. Unless we succeed, our race will soon vanish from this planet. Only the City will remain.'

10

The City Attacks

Dan Galloway smashed a football-sized chunk of rock from the big boulder with a swing of his pick-axe and passed it over to Jill Tarrant who began chipping it into smaller chunks with her hammer, and sorting out the pieces showing the silvery gleam of the Parrinium ore. For some reason the Parrinium vein ran through the rocks in a kind of inner stripe, so that a good deal of rock had to be smashed to get at it. With automated mining equipment it would have been simple enough, but working by hand it was a back-breaking and tedious business.

Most of it was being done by the three humans. Terrified as they were of the Daleks, the Exxilons lacked the capacity for methodical, organised tasks of this kind, and worked slowly and inefficiently. When the Daleks discovered that threats simply made them work less efficiently than ever, they had ordered the three humans to join in the digging. Galloway had blustered and protested, but in the end he had set to work with the others. There was no alternative. Much of the Parrinium-bearing rock had been covered by drifting sand, and the Exxilons had been put to work digging down to it. They had dug out an enormous pit in the sand in their efforts to reach the ore.

Three Daleks supervised the digging from a vantage point high on the dunes. Soon the Dalek leader appeared from the direction of the ship, and joined them for a conference. He had left the fifth Dalek, the expedition's scientist, hard at work in the ship's laboratory. 'Explosive charges will shortly be completed,' he announced importantly. 'They must be placed on the beacon on the summit of the City and then detonated. A Dalek patrol will enter the City to investigate scientific installations while the charges are being positioned.'

'Agreed.' This was the second in command. 'Will destruction of the beacon restore electrical energy to the ship?'

'Logic circuits suggest this is the source of interference.'

There was a sudden commotion below them, and the Exxilons at the bottom of the pit began climbing from the hole with shrill cries of panic. One of the Daleks glided down the dune towards them. 'Return to work or you will be exterminated!'

The panic-stricken Exxilons dashed past, and began scrambling up the face of the dune.

Intrigued by the commotion, Galloway, Hamilton and Jill Tarrant ran to the edge of the crater and looked down. Nearly all the Exxilons had fled by now, and only one solitary straggler was still climbing desperately up the side of the pit.

Puzzled, Jill stared down into the crater. There seemed to be no reason for the sudden panic—then she noticed that the sand at the bottom was *rippling*, as if something underneath was struggling to get out ...

Suddenly an enormous metal snake shot out of the sand and reared high in the air. The lens set into the blunt head glowed like a single fiery eye.

Peter Hamilton reached down to help the cowering Exxilon worker, but it was too late. The metal snake reared up, hovered for a moment then lunged at the terrified Exxilon. There was a sizzle of power and the Exxilon screamed and fell back dead into the crater.

Hamilton and the others backed hurriedly away, just as the first of the Daleks appeared and opened fire.

If any of the bullets hit the metal snake, they failed to harm it. It lunged forward in a blur of speed, blasting at the Dalek with an energy-bolt. The Dalek spun round, rushed blindly forwards, then toppled over the edge of the crater, smoke billowing from its metal casing. As the Dalek exploded, the snake retreated into the sand as quickly as it had come. High on his dune, Jebal turned and scuttled away.

Sarah's head nodded on her chest as Bellal's voice droned on and on. The Doctor had developed an obsessive curiosity about the City, and he was engaged in pumping Bellal for every possible scrap of information. Half-dozing, Sarah saw that Bellal was scratching in the cave floor with a pointed stone. 'This is the design, Doctor,' he was saying. 'Though I do not understand why it is of interest to you.'

'All knowledge is valuable,' said the Doctor. 'And as a matter of fact these signs are particularly interesting. Just look at this, Sarah.'

'What?' Sarah shook her head to wake herself up.

'Bellal says markings like these are cut into the walls of the City.'

'That's right, I saw them myself. Do they mean anything?'

'Indeed they do, Sarah. And I've seen them before too.'

'Where?'

'On the walls of a temple in Peru!'

'That's impossible.'

The Doctor beamed. 'That's what they said about the Peruvian temple. It's one of the great mysteries of Earth. All your scientists said no primitive race could possibly have built such a structure. Well now we've solved the mystery.'

'We have?'

The Doctor turned to Bellal. 'You said your ancestors were space travellers when Earth was still primitive?'

'That is so.'

'Then they must have visited the Earth at some period and taught its people to build. They left traces of their culture behind them.'

Sarah found it difficult to share the Doctor's enthusiasm. 'This is all very fascinating, but it isn't going to help us get off this planet. What about the power-drain? What causes that?'

The Doctor smiled. 'I'm coming to that, Sarah. The City gets its energy in two ways—through roots in the ground, and by absorbing it directly from the air. As soon as anything on the planet produces energy, the City drains that energy from the atmosphere—my guess is that it's done by that beacon on the tower.'

'And that's what mucked up the TARDIS?'

'Well, putting it crudely, yes. So, what we have to do is—'

One of Bellal's people came running into the cave. 'One of the machine creatures at the diggings has been destroyed by a probe.'

Bellal was not surprised. 'The City must see the mining as a threat. It is fighting back.'

The Doctor said, 'Well, I must say it's being quite helpful at the moment. So another of our Dalek friends has been disposed of, eh?' He got to his feet. 'Come on, Sarah. We'll take a look at this City. Bellal, will you be our guide?'

At the Parrinium diggings an agitated conference was taking place. After repeated threats of extermination from the Daleks, the Exxilon workers had been herded together again. But they flatly refused to resume work at the same site, insisting that it was too close to the City. Not even Dalek machine-guns could make them change their minds.

At last the Daleks had been forced to give way, and a new deposit, much further from the City, had been located. Now the Daleks were about to send the workers on their way.

The Dalek leader's eye-stalk swivelled towards Jill Tarrant. 'The female will go with Exxilon workers. Male humans will remain here.'

Peter Hamilton moved to Jill's side, and put a protective arm around her shoulders. 'Oh no you don't. We stay together.'

Immediately, Dalek machine-guns swung round to cover him. 'Obey, or you will both be exterminated.'

Jill Tarrant moved away. 'It's all right, Peter, some-one's got to sort out the ore. Don't worry, I can take care of myself.'

Peter Hamilton knew there was no alternative. He had to obey, or die. He moved over to Galloway, and Jill went over to the group of Exxilons.

The Dalek leader turned to the remaining Daleks. 'Patrol will now leave. Two Daleks will enter City and carry out scientific survey.'

'We obey.' Two of the Daleks moved off.

The leader swung round on the remaining Dalek. 'Male humans will accompany you to the City tower.'

Galloway scowled at the Dalek leader. 'Why us?'

The Dalek leader indicated four small metal cylinders with instruments set into the top. They had been brought from the Dalek ship some time ago, and piled up close to the diggings. A roll of magnetic tape lay beside them. 'You will carry explosive charges to City and fix them in position around the beacon.'

Hamilton looked ironically at Galloway. 'It seems they want us to do their dirty work for them. You're in command. What do we do?'

'We do what we're told,' snarled Galloway. Under his breath he added, 'For the moment!'

The Dalek leader moved off after the working party and Galloway picked up two cylinders.

Pocketing the roll of magnetic tape, Hamilton did the same. Followed by their Dalek guard, they set off towards the City.

The Dalek leader turned to Jill Tarrant and the group of Exxilon slaves. 'Work will commence at new diggings immediately. Move!'

*

The Doctor stood at the edge of the rocky plain and stared admiringly up at the towering white bulk of the City. 'There's no doubt about it, that must be one of the seven hundred wonders of the Universe.'

'Wait till you get closer,' said Sarah. 'It's even more impressive.'

'I'm sure it is. But you're not going any closer—not this time.'

'Now look here, Doctor—'

Cutting across her protest the Doctor said, 'I've got a very important job for you to do.'

'You're not just trying to get rid of me?'

'Certainly not. Remember if the Earth ship doesn't get away from here with the Parrinium, millions of people in the outer worlds are going to die.'

'What do you want me to do?'

'Contact the Earth expedition and make Galloway co-operate. Somehow he's got to load a supply of Parrinium into his ship, and be ready to blast off the instant power is restored. And remember, the Daleks will get their power back too, and they'll do everything they can to stop the Earth ship taking off. I know the Daleks of old, and they're definitely not medical missionaries.'

Bellal had gone on ahead, and he was waving impatiently. 'Bellal seems to be getting worried, Doctor. You'd better be off.'

'One more thing, Sarah,' said the Doctor awkwardly. 'If by any chance I don't get back you must return to Earth with the expedition. At least it will be your own world, if not your own time. Sorry I got you into all this.'

Before Sarah could answer, he turned and hurried after Bellal.

It was a long and tiring journey across the baking heat of the rocky plain. Bellal moved surprisingly quickly, darting across the sun-baked rock like a lizard, and it was all the Doctor could do to keep up with him. They reached the City wall at last, and the Doctor stood staring in admiration at the gleaming white walls that towered above him. 'It's beautiful,' he breathed.

'To you, perhaps, Doctor. To me it is only evil. It sucks the life from our planet.'

The Doctor put an ear close to the wall, heard the distant hum of mighty machinery. He touched one of the white bricks, and it glowed briefly into life beneath his fingers. 'Touch-sensitised. Brilliant. Simply brilliant.'

Bellal led the way along to another section of wall. 'You wanted to see the symbols. Here they are.'

The Doctor followed Bellal and gazed in fascination at the Aztec-like symbols carved deep into the walls. 'My belief is that they form some kind of message,' said Bellal. 'I have tried many times to interpret them, but the old knowledge is all lost. Do they hold any meaning for you?'

'Perhaps,' murmured the Doctor. 'Perhaps. Are there any more? Surely there must be more?'

'They continue here,' Bellal led the way to an alcove set in the wall. It was just big enough for the two of them to enter, and it was covered with the strange symbols. This time they were low enough to touch. The

Doctor studied them. 'I think I'm on to something here. This is a kind of intelligence test. One of these symbols doesn't conform . . .'

Bellal watched for a moment as the Doctor brooded over the complex symbols, occasionally reaching out to run his fingers over them. Feeling there was nothing he could do to help, Bellal went to the edge of the alcove to look around. Two Daleks were heading along the wall, coming straight towards him. Panic-stricken, Bellal ducked back. 'Daleks, Doctor—coming this way!'

The Doctor peered out, and a burst of Dalek machine-gun fire whizzed past his nose.

He jumped back, pulling Bellal with him.

Bellal was chattering with fear. 'We're trapped, Doctor. Trapped! As soon as they arrive they'll shoot us down—and there is nowhere to run!'

The Trap

The Doctor stared at the symbol-covered wall, thinking furiously. What Bellal said was true enough. If they left the alcove they would be exposed to the Daleks' fire. It was hopeless trying to run. The bare white walls and the rocky plain offered not a scrap of cover. For the moment the alcove protected them, but as soon as the Daleks arrived . . .

He stared at the carved symbols. 'Do be quiet, old chap. I'm trying to concentrate.'

The Daleks swung round into the alcove, machine-guns blazing. They sprayed every inch of the confined space with bullets—and suddenly stopped firing. Their eye-stalks swivelled round in almost ludicrous surprise.

The alcove was empty.

Bellal was scarcely able to believe he was still alive. 'What did you do, Doctor?'

'Pressed the right button, it seems. I simply picked out the symbol that didn't fit, and traced its outline with my finger.'

'And that made the door slide open?'

The Doctor shrugged. 'I can't imagine what else.'

Bellal looked round, taking in his surroundings. They were in a small, bare, white-walled room. Humanoid skeletons lay sprawled about the floor. Bellal stared at them in horror. 'Doctor, what is this place? Can we get out again?'

The Doctor nodded towards the skeletons. 'I'm not sure. *They* didn't.'

'Then we have entered another trap?'

The Doctor rubbed his chin. 'It can't be. That wouldn't make sense.'

Bellal gestured towards the twisted skeleton forms. 'These must have been trapped, just as we were. Some of them may have lain here for centuries.'

The Doctor was thinking aloud. 'Yes . . . they passed the first intelligence test, and got this far . . . and failed to pass the second!'

'What test?'

'I'm not sure. But there's got to be one. It's only logical!'

His back to the sliding door that had admitted them —a door which had now completely disappeared—the Doctor walked across the room, picking his way across the gleaming white bones of those who had gone before him. He stopped at the opposite wall, raised his hand and pressed his palm against the smooth white surface. Immediately the wall lit up, revealing an immensely complicated design. 'Splendid, just as I thought!'

'I don't understand, Doctor. This is just a pattern on the wall.'

'No, no, it's much more than that. It's a maze . . . a test of skill and logic that we have to solve before we can move further into the City.'

'And if we fail?'

'Presumably we stay here till we become like our bony friends.' The Doctor brooded over the maze. 'Now then, point of entry *here*, exit point *here*. Since the

96

walls are touch-sensitised, I imagine that I simply have to move my finger along the correct route.' The Doctor stared at the maze in total concentration. Something told him that he would only be given one chance. If his finger strayed from the correct path, the maze pattern would fade, and the exit door be closed forever.

He put his finger on the starting point and began moving it slowly through the maze.

Meanwhile in the alcove, the two Daleks were tackling the problem of gaining entry to the City. Not with a single intuitive flash, like the Doctor, but with slow, remorseless Dalek logic.

The first Dalek scanned the pattern with its eye-stick. 'Computer indicates that symbols contain simple logic test. We must deduce which symbol does not conform to the others.'

The second Dalek too was methodically scanning the pattern. 'I will run computer check. All symbols have now been registered.' There was a faint whirring, clicking sound as the Dalek's inner computer processed the information. Then it announced triumphantly. 'Non-conforming symbol now isolated.' With its sucker-arm it indicated one of the symbols. 'This is key symbol.'

The first Dalek glided closer to the wall and began tracing the outline of the symbol with its sucker-arm. There was a hum of hidden machinery and a door started to slide smoothly open.

'There!' said the Doctor triumphantly. His finger moved to the maze exit, the pattern faded and a door slid back revealing a long white corridor. Bellal hung back in fear. Suddenly the door by which they'd first entered started to open. 'Come along,' said the Doctor. 'The Daleks are close behind us.' They stepped into the corridor, and the door closed behind them.

A moment later the Daleks were in the room. Their eye-sticks swivelled to and fro. 'Scan the walls,' ordered the first Dalek. 'We must locate next access point!'

The corridor went on and on for what seemed a very long way—then suddenly it widened out into a kind of hall. The floor changed too. A complex pattern of glowing red and white tiles marked with strange symbols stretched across their path. Bellal would have hurried across it, but the Doctor held him back. 'Stay where you are.'

'What is it?'

'Another test, I think. The people who built this place were hardly likely to go in for ornamental flooring just for the sake of it.'

Bellal shook his head wearily. Ever since entering the City they seemed to have been beset by new and terrifying dangers. 'I don't understand. What must we do this time?'

The Doctor smiled. 'Ever played Venusian hop-scotch? No, of course you haven't.' He produced his sonic screwdriver, and made a quick adjustment. 'This is where we cheat a little.' He knelt by the pattern and began scanning the tiles one by one. The sonic screwdriver gave out a low buzzing sound, which occasionally shot up to a higher pitch. The Doctor stepped on to one of the red squares, and knelt to test the tiles in front of him. 'Now then, I want you to follow me exactly. Step on the same squares as I do—and on no others.' The Doctor took another step forward, and turned to guide Bellal. 'That's right, old chap, take it steady. The red one first . . . now jump two squares to that white one . . . that's it, good . . .' Step by step the Doctor led Bellal through the pattern, weaving his way across the chessboard of red and white squares. With a final leap, he reached the other side, and reached out to help Bellal to safety. 'One last jump, old chap. There, that's it!' He slapped the baffled little Exxilon on the back. 'Here we are. Jolly little game, don't you think?'

'I do not understand, Doctor,' said Bellal irritably. 'Was all that really necessary?'

'Oh, I think so,' said the Doctor. He fished in his pocket, produced an old coin and examined it. 'Do I need five piastres? No, of course I don't. Just you watch this!' The Doctor tossed the coin on to the giant chessboard, choosing a square they *hadn't* stepped on. There was a fierce crackle of electrical power, a shower of sparks, and a sudden explosion. The smoke cleared and the Doctor said, 'Look!' The little coin had been fused into a shapeless blob of metal. 'That might have been us, Bellal—now let's go and see what other pleasures they have in store for us!'

The door slid open, and the two Daleks emerged cautiously into the corridor. 'Proceed with all caution,' commanded the first Dalek. 'This territory will be classified as hostile.'

'Understood.'

The Daleks moved slowly on, coming at last to the

broad hall with its pattern of chequered tiles. Since Daleks take no interest in the finer points of interior decoration, they failed to see anything unusual in the red and white chequered pattern on the floor of the hall. The first Dalek glided straight on to it—and was hurled back with a fierce crackle of sparks.

The second Dalek reacted instantly, firing a series of sweeping bursts that riddled the chessboard pattern with bullets, exploding most of the deadly electrical circuits beneath it. The Dalek sped across the smoking floor in a determined rush, and came to a halt at the other side. It turned and scanned its wounded colleague. It was weaving dazedly to and fro, smoke pouring from the bottom of its casing. 'Damage report,' ordered the second Dalek.

'Non-conductive shielding partially burnt-out. Sensors record massive electrical charge. No serious damage—am able to proceed.' The wounded Dalek crossed the exploded floor to join its fellow. With a note of satisfaction it reported, 'Weapon designed to destroy humanoid tissue. Ineffective against superior Dalek shielding. We will continue.'

The recovered Dalek glided on, but the first Dalek ordered, 'Wait. Observe. We must gather scientific data.' The bullet-riddled floor was repairing itself before their very eye-stalks, the damaged tiles regenerating themselves into their former pattern of red and white. The Daleks observed the spectacle unimpressed. 'Note that City has self-regeneration faculties,' ordered the first Dalek. 'Proceed.'

The Daleks moved remorselessly on.

*

The Doctor and Bellal found that the corridor they were following ended in a blank wall—but as they approached the wall, a door slid back to admit them to a bare white-walled room much like the one by which they had entered the City—though this one at least had no skeletons littering the floor.

Bellal gazed round despairingly. 'We make no progress, Doctor.'

'Don't be too sure. Moving through this City is like being inside a living thing—in its bloodstream, rather than its stomach, I hope! We're being passed along like invading microbes. But all the time we're moving nearer the heart.'

As darkness began to fall, and the eerie fog seemed to rise out of the ground, Sarah decided it was time to make a move. She slid out of the little hollow she had dug for herself in the sand, and peered cautiously over the top of the dune.

Work on the diggings had stopped as darkness came down, and now the black-robed Exxilon slave-workers were huddled round a low fire. A little way from the fire, Sarah could see Jill Tarrant, leaning back wearily against the lower slopes of a dune. She seemed to be dozing. There was no sign of Galloway or Hamilton.

A single Dalek sentry was patrolling the site of the diggings, gliding around the perimeter of the area on a regular circuit.

It was this sentry which had been delaying Sarah's mission. There was no chance of contacting the Earth expedition in daylight, without being spotted, so Sarah had made herself a hiding place in the sand and caught up with her sleep. Now it was time to move.

She slid quietly down the side of the dune, freezing whenever the Dalek sentry came in sight. A final dash brought her close to the dozing girl. 'Jill,' she whispered. 'Psst! Jill! Can you hear me?'

Jill Tarrant's head jerked up. 'Sarah? Where are you?'

'Just behind you. Keep your voice down, and don't look at me when you talk.'

Flat on her stomach, Sarah wriggled closer to Jill, using the girl's body to shield her from the Dalek.

'What happened to you?' whispered Jill. 'Where's the Doctor?'

'He's gone to the City. He's going to try and switch off that beacon. He thinks it's causing the power-block. Where are the others?'

'No idea. The Daleks kept them behind and sent me off here.'

'The Doctor sent me here with a message for you all —but if the others aren't here . . .'

'We shall have to manage without them,' said Jill determinedly. 'What does he want us to do?'

'Somehow you've got to get the Parrinium into your ship, and be ready for take-off when the power comes back on. How much Parrinium have you found?'

Jill gestured to a pile of filled sacks. 'More than enough. The concentration here is incredibly high. When it's processed back on Earth that ore will yield enough Parrinium to end the space plague for good.'

'Somehow we've got to find a way of getting it on to your ship,' said Sarah thoughtfully.

'With a Dalek standing guard?'

'I know ... but we've still got to try. Just let me think for a moment.'

Sarah lay still, looking at her watch, and studying the movements of the patrolling Dalek. It was carrying out its patrol in the systematic manner so typical of the Dalek mentality, covering the same route at the same speed on every circuit.

Sarah made a final calculation and said, 'Right, that's it!'

'What is?'

'I've been timing that sentry. It takes about twenty minutes to do the full circuit—and for over half the time it's out of sight behind the dunes.'

'So?'

'Well, if we can't see it, it can't see us. We've got ten minutes in every twenty to work unseen. Now then, have you got any empty sacks?'

Jill nodded. 'There's a huge pile just over there. We're supposed to go on mining tomorrow. Why?'

'As soon as the Dalek's out of sight you sneak over and get them. Wait till I give the word.' Sarah paused, watching the Dalek. 'Right—now!'

The Dalek disappeared behind the dune, and Jill sprinted for the sacks. She returned with a pile of them in a matter of minutes and by the time the Dalek reappeared she was leaning innocently against the dune again.

'Right,' whispered Sarah. 'Now, as soon as the Dalek's out of sight, we start filling these empty sacks with sand. We want a pile as big as the pile of Parrinium sacks.'

'But we can only work half the time,' protested Jill. 'It'll take all night.'

'Then we'd better get on with it, hadn't we?' Sarah began scooping sand into one of the empty sacks with her hands.

12

The Nightmare

The Doctor abandoned his search of the room in some disgust. 'Nothing! Not a single clue. And yet every part of our route through this City has been carefully planned. This room must be here for a purpose.'

'Perhaps we have come as far as we are permitted?' suggested Bellal. 'Ought we to turn back?'

'No, it would be fatal to give up—literally so, I imagine. We'll just have to start again.'

Patiently the Doctor took up the search, running his hand over every inch of walls and floor that he could reach, trying to discover some clue to the next test. Dispiritedly Bellal did the same, though he didn't really expect to succeed where the Doctor had failed.

Yet in a way it was Bellal who found the solution. He ran his hands over a section of wall already checked once by the Doctor. This time the wall did respond. A tiny point of light appeared on its surface. Bellal was about to call the Doctor when the light began pulsing in a regular rhythm. Bellal found he could neither speak nor take his eyes from it.

The Doctor finished examining a section of wall for the third time. He shook his head. 'I've got a funny feeling that somehow I'm missing the point of all this . . .'

Bellal didn't answer. The Doctor turned and saw that

the little Exxilon was creeping towards him, arms out-stretched like a sleepwalker, hands curved into talons. Before the Doctor could react, Bellal launched himself across the room and seized him by the throat. The Doctor grabbed the Exxilon's wrists and tried to pull them away. But Bellal was filled with unnatural strength, and the Doctor realised that he was fighting the City itself. He stared deep into Bellal's glowing eyes and shouted, 'Bellal, don't! Remember where we are, and why we came here. Think! We're in the City, Bellal. I am your friend. Your friend!'

Slowly the mad glare faded from Bellal's eyes. 'What . . . what happened?' he sobbed.

The Doctor patted him on the back. 'All right, old chap, it's all over now. What's the last thing you remember?'

'There was this light . . . it kept flashing . . .'

'Testing our ability to deal with mind control, I imagine—and look, we seem to have passed the test!'

A door was opening in the wall ahead of them. The Doctor looked down at Bellal. 'Do you feel ready to go on?'

'No . . .' said Bellal wearily. 'But I know that we must.'

They passed through the door, and it closed behind them.

A few minutes later the Daleks entered the empty room.

Although it was dark now, the periodic flashes from the beacon lit up the area with unnatural clarity. Hamilton and Galloway stood gazing up at the impressive height of the tower. Built against the outer wall of the City, the tower was constructed rather like a child's pile of bricks. An immense slab of stone formed the base, on top stood a slightly smaller slab, on top of that another still smaller slab, and so on until the topmost cube of stone which housed the beacon itself. Because of this construction the tower narrowed as it rose, and each of the four sides formed an immense flight of steps.

Galloway turned to their Dalek guard. 'We're supposed to go up there?'

'The climb is well within human capability. When you reach the summit you will place explosive charges beneath the beacon.'

Hamilton looked up at the great flashing light that hung in the sky so far above them. Were they really supposed to destroy it with these four little metal cylinders? 'Suppose we refuse to make the climb?'

'The girl will be exterminated. You will obey.'

Hamilton looked at Dan Galloway, who nodded abruptly. They moved over to the base of the tower. 'You will be in range of my fire at all times,' warned the Dalek. 'Bomb-timing devices are already set. You will activate them and descend the tower. Do this and your lives will be spared.'

'Let's get on with it,' said Galloway wearily. He put down the two bomb cylinders, and Hamilton did the same. By standing on tiptoe, Hamilton could just reach the edge of the bottom step. 'You'll have to give me a leg up, Dan.'

Galloway crouched down until Hamilton could get a foot on his shoulder, then slowly straightened up, hoisting him on to the first ledge. Once Hamilton was up there, Galloway passed him the four bombs, one by one. When they were safely on the ledge, Hamilton reached down and heaved Galloway up beside him. 'There you are then,' he said grimly. 'We do that a few hundred times and we'll be at the top!'

Watched by the patrolling Dalek, they began the ascent of the next ledge.

The smooth white corridors stretched on and on. Bellal looked up at the Doctor, who was walking calmly ahead, apparently untired, and unafraid. Bellal, who was both, said hopefully, 'We've come quite a long way without any tests, Doctor.'

'I think we must be getting close to the centre of the City.'

'Perhaps we are safe now?'

'I wouldn't count on it. Has it occurred to you to wonder why the City is testing us like this?'

'What do you mean?'

'The City could have destroyed us a hundred times by now. Instead it's given us an opportunity to survive, by continually proving our intelligence.'

'That is so,' agreed Bellal. 'But what is its purpose in doing this?'

'Perhaps by passing the tests we show we have an intelligence-level that could be useful. We might have knowledge that it can add to its data-banks for instance.'

'And afterwards?'

'The one thing that menaces the City is the development of any outside intelligence on the planet. I believe it lures any intelligent beings inside with its tests—and once it has taken their knowledge, it destroys them.'

'Then I was right after all. We have entered a trap.'

'Perhaps so. But remember, traps can be made to open as well as close.'

Suddenly they came to a dead-end.

The lights in the corridor began to pulse. Strange whirling colours began flashing before their eyes, and the air was filled with discordant electronic noises.

'What is it, Doctor?' cried Bellal. 'What's happening?'

'I think it's the ultimate test—an assault on our sanity! Resist it, Bellal. Try to block it from your mind.'

Reality began to blur and shimmer round them as walls and floor began spinning into twisted, writhing multi-coloured shapes. Electronic shrieks howled through their brains, making thought impossible. Bellal dropped to the floor. Arms wrapped round his head and knees drawn up to his chin, he rolled himself into a tight ball, trying vainly to shut out the lights and the sounds.

The Doctor however forced himself to stare unblinkingly into the screaming vortex of madness. 'You are an illusion,' he shouted. 'You have no substance, no truth. You do not exist. *You do not exist!*'

There was utter silence. The swirling lights disappeared, the sounds cut off, walls and floor returned to solid reality. The Doctor helped Bellal to get up. 'It's all right,' he said gently. 'It's over now.'

Bellal's eyes were staring over the Doctor's shoulder. 'Look, Doctor,' he breathed.

The Doctor turned. A door slid back in the wall before them, revealing an enormous control room. It was lined with complex instrument panels and dominated by one central console. There was a chair before this console and in it a white-robed figure. It sat motionless, regarding them, eyes bright in the mummified face beneath the hood.

'The last survivor,' whispered the Doctor. 'Perhaps the City kept him here to serve it.' He took a step nearer and the wizened figure shimmered, blurred, and dissolved into a pile of dust. Bellal jumped back with a cry of horror.

'Our fault, I'm afraid,' said the Doctor. 'Our entry set up an air current—and that was enough to break the surface tension that held him together.'

The door closed behind them, blocking their escape. Bellal looked at the banks of complex instruments.

'Is this the heart of the City?'

'The heart, the brain, and the nervous system. This is what we have to destroy.'

Bellal lowered his voice in awe. 'For thousands of years the City has defied all attempts to harm it. Can we really end its power?'

The Doctor too was looking round. 'I think there *is* a way. But to destroy it, I must first know more about it.' He began moving about the room, studying the complex instrument panels, whirling dials and luminous gauges with absorbed attention.

Bellal looked on, feeling as usual a little lost. He knew he could never hope to understand the complex science of his ancestors. He wandered over to the far side of the wall, where a number of translucent screens were set into the wall. As he stared at them, they slowly became transparent. They seemed like windows to another room adjoining the one they were in, an immense shadowy room filled with swirling mists.

Bellal stared into the mist in fascination. As he watched, strange, monstrous shapes started forming behind the screens . . .

13

The Antibodies

Bellal sprang back in alarm. 'Doctor, come quickly.'

The Doctor came over to him, and they both stood staring in fascination. The giant shapes were larger now, more distinct, and they were beginning to take on a vaguely humanoid form. 'I'm afraid we have less time than I thought,' said the Doctor gravely.

'What is it, Doctor? What's happening?'

'The City is creating these creatures to protect itself—like antibodies. I think it has decided we're a danger to it, so it's devising means to neutralise us.' He turned away, reaching for his sonic screwdriver. 'Keep an eye on them for me, Bellal. Warn me when they seem to be—complete.' Hurrying to the central computer terminal, the Doctor began dismantling the control panel.

Ignoring the pain in his aching muscles, Peter Hamilton dragged himself on to the topmost ledge of the beacon tower. Gasping for breath he reached down and took the bombs Galloway passed up to him, stowing them well away from the edge. Then with one final heave, he helped Galloway to scramble on to the ledge beside him. For a moment the two men lay there gasping, recovering from the tremendous effort of the climb. It had been a nightmarish business, all the worse because it had been so repetitive. They had repeated the same set of actions over and over again, working themselves, and the bombs, up the endless ledges.

Now, at last, they had reached the top. Every few seconds the glare of the flashing beacon lit up the area for miles around. They could see the sprawling white buildings and towers of the City, and the bare rocky plain all around. Far below was the tiny figure of the watchful Dalek, waiting for them to complete their mission and come down.

Hamilton looked up. The beacon itself was set upon a kind of metallic framework rather like a miniature Eiffel Tower, which rose out of the block on which they were standing. 'Four supporting legs, four bombs,' said Hamilton. 'Come on, let's fix a bomb on each one and then get down.'

He fished the magnetic tape from his pocket and used it to lash the bomb to the first support. He raised the detonating section, flicked it into activity and thrust home the activating plunger. Working his way round the ledge he fixed the second bomb and the third. He waited for Galloway to pass him the fourth and last bomb, but Galloway shook his head. 'No. Not this one.'

Look, that Dalek is watching every move we make.'

Determinedly Galloway tucked the last little cylinder inside his tunic. 'It can't make out details at this range. Three charges will bring down the beacon just as well as four. This is the only weapon we've got, and we're taking it back with us. Now come on. Those bombs are ticking, remember.' Galloway dropped down on to the ledge below, and Hamilton followed him. At least it would be easier going down.

He wondered what Galloway planned to do with the bomb ...

Night on Exxilon is short, and the first signs of dawn were appearing in the sky, as the Dalek came round the dune on its final circuit. The Exxilon slave-workers were already shuffling towards the diggings, and the Dalek glided up to the Earth girl, who lay sleeping beneath her blanket.

'Work will re-commence at dawn. Move!'

There was no response.

'Move!' repeated the Dalek angrily. It extended its sucker-arm and twitched the blanket away—to reveal a pile of sand shaped roughly into human form. 'The human female has escaped. I have failed, I have failed. She must be located.' The Dalek began a frantic search of the area, but Jill Tarrant was gone.

Bellal looked uneasily at the figures behind the screens. They were almost complete now, giant lumpy versions of the basic humanoid form with massive limbs and blurred, shapeless features. They looked like huge clay men brought to hideous life. They stirred ... Bellal called, 'Doctor, I think we should go now!'

The Doctor looked up from a maze of dismantled and reassembled circuitry. 'All right, Bellal, nearly finished.'

Bellal went over to watch him. 'What are you trying to do?'

'There's no time to find and isolate the beacon circuits as I'd hoped. So I'm using a kind of psychological warfare. I'm trying to confuse the City's brain, engineer what humans would call a nervous break-down.'

'Will that have the same effect?'

The Doctor cross-connected another circuit. 'I hope so. A computer is a thing of logic. It can't cope with paradox.'

Bellal stood watching the Doctor at work. He didn't notice that the huge forms behind the screens had come fully alive, and that the screens were sliding silently back.

The two Daleks had endured a battery of mind-bending lights and sounds with stolid indifference. Daleks have so little imagination that it is almost impossible to hypnotise them. Eventually the effects had died away, and a door had slid open before them. The Daleks glided swiftly through.

Just as the Doctor finished his task, an enormous, shape-less hand fell on Bellal's shoulder, gripping it with crushing force. One of the giant zombies had him in its grip. He screamed and the Doctor grabbed Bellal's other arm and pulled him free. They began backing away, as the creature lurched slowly towards them. More of the giant zombies came forward, forming a menacing semi-circle in front of the Doctor and Bellal.

They retreated further and further across the control room, dodging between the banks of instruments. The leading zombie found its way blocked by a computer terminal, and smashed it aside with a single sweep of its club-like arm. Other zombie creatures rampaged through the control room, destroying everything that stood in their path.

Lights began flashing on and off erratically and there was a whine of tortured machinery. The Doctor wondered if it was a result of his own efforts or the damage caused by the antibodies themselves. Not that it mattered very much. By now they were trapped against a blank wall with zombies lurching closer and closer, huge hands outstretched. There was no escape.

Once again the Doctor was saved by his enemies. The door opened and two Daleks glided into the room. At the sight of the Doctor they gave a triumphant cry of 'Exterminate!' and opened fire.

The Doctor and Bellal threw themselves down. Dalek machine-gun bullets ripped across the room, thudding into the massive bodies of the zombies. The creatures turned and began lumbering towards their new enemies.

The Daleks fired a series of frantic bursts, but their bullets had little effect. The zombies hesitated for a moment, as the bullets struck them, and then lurched forward to the attack.

'Quick, Bellal,' shouted the Doctor. 'Now's our chance.' They began moving around the edge of the battle. 'Halt! Do not move!' screamed one of the Daleks. It swung round to fire at the Doctor, but suddenly the leading zombie was upon it. It seized the Dalek's gun-stick in one colossal hand and slowly bent it up into the shape of a letter U. The Doctor and Bellal dashed through the still-open door.

They hurtled down the corridor at frantic speed, until they reached one of the sliding doors that had barred their way in. It was opening and shutting erratically. 'The City controls are breaking down,' said the Doctor exultantly. 'It's working, Bellal! With any luck the other traps won't be operating either! Come on!' They hared on down the corridor.

In the computer control room, the Daleks were falling back before the zombie attack. Their cries of 'Exterminate!' gave way to frantic screams of 'Retreat! Retreat!' Spinning round, they shot through the open door in pursuit of the Doctor and Bellal. Remorselessly, the zombie antibodies lumbered after them.

Unharmed and unhindered, Doctor and Bellal passed the nightmare room, the electrified pavement, and the room full of skeletons and arrived at last in the alcove through which they'd entered the City. Bellal collapsed gasping against the wall. 'I never believed we would escape, Doctor.'

'Never say die, Bellal,' said the Doctor. 'Mind you the battle's not over yet. The Daleks will do everything in their power to stop the Earth mission from getting off the planet. Come on, we'd better see what we can do to help.' Apparently unaffected by their ordeals, the Doctor set off briskly across the rocks. With a groan Bellal heaved himself upright and staggered after him.

Their Dalek guard close behind them, Hamilton and Galloway trudged towards the mining area. Galloway was still hugging the bomb beneath his coat. He had been silent and morose on the long journey back, and Hamilton wondered again what he was planning. He took a quick glance at his wrist-chronometer, wondering how long before the bombs they'd set on the beacon were due to detonate.

The Dalek leader came forward to meet their guard. 'Report.'

'Explosive devices now in position. Detonation will occur shortly, and power will be restored.'

'Prepare for immediate take-off,' ordered the leader.

Peter Hamilton looked round. The Exxilon slaves were still filling the last few bags, but there was no sign of Jill. 'Where's the girl you were holding?'

There was a brief silence. 'Come on,' demanded Hamilton. 'Tell me where she is.'

'She escaped during darkness. Now that our work is almost completed she is of no importance. You will load the Parrinium bags on to our ship. Move!'

The Doctor and Bellal arived at the edge of the dunes just in time to see Hamilton and Galloway carrying the last of the Parrinium bags towards the Dalek ship.

'The Daleks seem to be getting ready to leave,' said the Doctor thoughtfully. 'So they must be pretty confident they'll be able to blast off. I wonder what they've been up to?'

Bellal turned and looked behind them. The white towers of the City gleamed behind them, and the great beacon was still flashing. 'I think we have failed, Doctor. The City is unharmed. Soon it will repair the little damage we have done. Now the Daleks are leaving with the medicine the humans need, and we are powerless to stop them.'

'You're not being logical, Bellal,' said the Doctor

severely. 'If the City is undamaged, the Daleks can't leave. No, I think they must have—' He broke off suddenly. 'Get down!'

'What is it, Doctor?'

'Someone's coming up the other side of the dune . . .'

14

The Last Victory

Bellal crouched down. The Doctor peered over the top of the dunes—and jumped to his feet with a cry of delight. 'Sarah! Thank goodness you're safe.'

'Doctor!' Sarah came running up the dune, Jill Tarrant close behind her. There was a confused babble of greetings. 'Did you succeed, Doctor?' asked Sarah. 'Will we get the power back?'

The Doctor said ruefully, 'I'm not sure. It'll take time for the effects to show. What about you?'

Sarah said triumphantly, 'We've just got back from the Earth mission ship.'

'Everything's set for blast-off the minute we get full power,' said Jill. 'But we've still got to rescue Dan and Peter. I can't handle the ship on my own.'

The Doctor said, 'I'm afraid that's not going to be easy. They're heading for the Dalek ship!'

Hamilton and Galloway staggered up the ramp and dumped the last of the Parrinium sacks in the hold just inside the doorway. It had taken a number of trips to get all the bags on board. The Dalek leader was already at the control panel. Hamilton dumped his bags down any old how, but Galloway began stacking the bags neatly in the hold. What was he up to now, currying favour with the Daleks, thought Hamilton irritably. 'Come on, Dan,' he said. Galloway waved him away, and suddenly Hamilton realised what Galloway was doing. He still had the bomb—and if he could plant it somewhere on the Dalek ship . . .

The Dalek sentry was waiting at the bottom of the ramp. 'Where is your companion?'

'Your leader told him to stack the bags. He'll be out in a moment.'

The Dalek turned indifferently away. It was scanning the surrounding area, looking for the two Daleks who had gone to the City.

Hamilton sneaked another look at his wrist chronometer. Surely there couldn't be long to go . . .

Shading his eyes he looked at the still-flashing beacon —and it disappeared in a brilliant white flash. The thunder of the distant explosion rolled across the dunes to the Dalek ship.

The Dalek leader saw the lights flash up on its control panel, checked that power was back and glided to the top of the ramp.

'Full power is now restored. You will board the ship.'

The sentry Dalek moved up the ramp and followed its leader into the control room. The Dalek leader made a rapid check of the control panel.

'We shall now commence the power build-up for blast-off.'

'The Dalek patrol has not yet reported back from the City.'

'Send urgent re-call signal.'

'No one is guarding the human captives. Shall I exterminate them?'

'Not necessary. They will perish like all other life on this planet.'

The Doctor and his companions were staring towards the City from their vantage point high in the dunes. The top of the tower was no more than a jagged stump. 'They've destroyed the beacon,' whispered Jill. 'Will that restore the power?'

'I think so, Jill. I'm afraid it looks as if the Daleks are going to get away with your Parrinium after all . . .'

'Doctor, there's something we haven't told you,' began Sarah.

A metallic voice came from behind them. 'Do not move or you will be exterminated.' They turned—

The two Daleks from the City had caught up with them. The Doctor noticed with wry amusement that the second Dalek's gun-stick was bent into an upward-pointing U, giving the Dalek a curiously drunken air. But the other Dalek's machine-gun was in full working order, and it was covering the little group at point-blank range. 'We shall go to the ship,' ordered the Dalek. 'Move!'

When they reached the ship they found Peter Hamilton waiting. The Dalek leader came out of the ship, and the two Daleks from the City went on board. The Doctor stared boldly at the Dalek leader, now left alone with the little group of captives. 'Well, don't prolong the agony. I presume you mean to kill us?'

'Such a death would be too easy, Doctor. You will stay on the planet and die in agony.'

'What makes you so sure?'

'As soon as we take off we shall bombard this area with space-plague missiles. You will be infected before you can reach the safety of your ships. You will all perish as a warning to those who oppose the plans of the Daleks.'

'What is your plan exactly?' asked the Doctor curiously. 'I take it your story of a plague on Dalek planets was pure invention?'

'Correct. Daleks are immune to the disease.'

'Then what do you want the Parrinium for?'

'When we hold all available supplies of Parrinium, all Earth colonies will surrender to the Daleks or perish from the space plague.'

'Don't you think Earth will send other missions?' asked Peter Hamilton defiantly. 'Now the power blockage is over we can have more ships here in no time.'

'I imagine the Daleks have taken that possibility into account, Peter,' said the Doctor. 'You're forgetting those space plague missiles.'

'Correct, Doctor. Before any Earth ship can arrive, the plague will have spread to contaminate the entire planet. Further landings will be impossible.'

The Dalek leader backed up the ramp, the doors closed behind it, and the ramp retracted. A low rumble of power came from the ship.

Peter Hamilton was staring up at the Dalek ship. 'What the blazes is Galloway up to? He should have planted that bomb and got off by now.'

Jill stared at him. 'You mean Galloway's still on there?'

'He was the last time I saw him. Unless he's managed to sneak off by some other way—and in that case, where is he?'

The rumble from the Dalek ship increased. 'No time

to look for him now,' said the Doctor. 'We'll be caught in the rocket exhaust if we don't get away from here.'

Followed by Bellal, the Doctor and Sarah ran for the dunes. Hamilton grabbed Jill's hand and pulled her after them. They climbed to the top of the nearest sand dune and watched the Dalek ship rise into the sky on a column of fire.

'Now, listen,' said the Doctor urgently. 'We must all get to our own ships and take off. There's just a chance we can get away before those missiles land.'

'But the Daleks have taken all the Parrinium,' shouted Peter. 'We must gather more.'

The Doctor shook his head. 'There's no time, young man—'

'It's all right,' said Sarah. 'The Daleks haven't got the Parrinium, you have! Jill and I loaded it on to your ship.'

Peter stared at her. 'But the bags we loaded on to the Dalek ship?'

'Sand,' said Sarah triumphantly. 'It took us all last night to fill them up.'

'Splendid,' said the Doctor. 'Very well done. Now, may I remind you we're still in danger of a very nasty death if we don't take off before they fire those missiles? Run for your ship, you two—now!'

As they began to run, Hamilton shouted to Jill, 'I should never have trusted Galloway. I should have set that bomb myself. He must have lost his nerve, surrendered to the Daleks . . .'

In the Dalek control room, the leader announced, 'Prepare to launch plague missiles.'

'I obey.' The Dalek glided to another part of the control room.

Hidden behind the stack of bags in the hold, Dan Galloway took the bomb from beneath his tunic, and set the timer to 'Instant'. He remembered the words of the dying Commander Stewart. A glory hunter, was he? Galloway drew a deep shuddering breath, and pressed home the plunger.

Haring across the dunes, the Doctor glanced up at the ascending Dalek ship—and saw it explode into a fireball in the sky. He stopped running. 'It's all right, everybody, no need to run. There's plenty of time now.'

A little later Hamilton came up to him. 'That was Dan Galloway,' he said softly.

The Doctor nodded. 'He could have set the bomb to delayed action, but the Daleks might have found it. I imagine he wanted to make sure.'

They climbed slowly to the top of the dune, and stood silent for a moment. The Doctor turned to Jill Tarrant and Peter Hamilton. 'Well, now it's up to you two to get the Parrinium to where it's needed.'

There was a sudden shout from Sarah who had turned to look at the City. 'Look, everyone!'

They all looked. Perhaps because of the Doctor's work on the computer, perhaps because of the Dalek assault on the beacon, perhaps even because of its own rampaging antibodies, the City was dying. Its clean-cut geometrical shapes were dissolving into shapeless blobs, melting and running away over the rocks. Sarah thought that it looked like some elaborate ice-cream sculpture, left exposed to the blazing heat of the sun.

'We succeeded after all,' whispered Bellal. 'The City is dead.'

'Rather a pity, in a way,' said the Doctor. 'Now there are only six hundred and ninety-nine wonders in the Universe!'

The Doctor and Sarah said their goodbyes, and headed for the TARDIS.

The Doctor rubbed his hands. 'Now for Florana, Sarah,' he said happily. 'I expect you feel like a little holiday after all this!'

'You can forget about Florana, Doctor,' said Sarah firmly. 'Just you concentrate on getting me home!'

SCIENCE FICTION

	0426200500	Terrance Dicks **STAR QUEST: SPACEJACK**	**60p**
	0426200748	Terrance Dicks **STAR QUEST: ROBOWORLD**	**75p**

'Doctor Who'

Δ	0426114558	Terrance Dicks **DOCTOR WHO AND THE ABOMINABLE SNOWMEN**	**70p**
Δ	0426200373	**DOCTOR WHO AND THE ANDROID INVASION**	**75p**
Δ	0426116313	Ian Marter **DOCTOR WHO AND THE ARK IN SPACE**	**70p**
Δ	0426112954	Terrance Dicks **DOCTOR WHO AND THE AUTON INVASION**	**75p**
Δ	0426116747	**DOCTOR WHO AND THE BRAIN OF MORBIUS**	**75p**
Δ	0426110250	**DOCTOR WHO AND THE CARNIVAL OF MONSTERS**	**70p**
Δ	042611471X	Malcolm Hulke **DOCTOR WHO AND THE CAVE-MONSTERS**	**70p**
Δ	0426117034	Terrance Dicks **DOCTOR WHO AND THE CLAWS OF AXOS**	**75p**
Δ	0426113160	David Whitaker **DOCTOR WHO AND THE CRUSADERS**	**70p**
Δ	0426114981	Brian Hayles **DOCTOR WHO AND THE CURSE OF PELADON**	**70p**
Δ	0426114639	Gerry Davis **DOCTOR WHO AND THE CYBERMEN**	**70p**
Δ	0426113322	Terrance Dicks **DOCTOR WHO AND THE DAEMONS**	**75p**
Δ	042611244X	**DOCTOR WHO AND THE DALEK INVASION OF EARTH**	**70p**
Δ	0426103807	**DOCTOR WHO AND THE DAY OF THE DALEKS**	**70p**
Δ	0426101103	David Whitaker **DOCTOR WHO AND THE DALEKS**	**70p**
Δ	0426119657	Terrance Dicks **DOCTOR WHO AND THE DEADLY ASSASSIN**	**60p**
Δ	042620042X	**DOCTOR WHO — DEATH TO THE DALEKS**	**75p**
Δ	0426200969	**DOCTOR WHO AND THE DESTINY OF THE DALEKS**	**75p**
Δ	0426108744	Malcolm Hulke **DOCTOR WHO AND THE DINOSAUR INVASION**	**75p**
Δ	0426103726	**DOCTOR WHO AND THE DOOMSDAY WEAPON**	**70p**

† For sale in Britain and Ireland only.
* Not for sale in Canada. • Reissues.
Δ Film & T.V. tie-ins.

SCIENCE FICTION

	*0426118421	**DOCTOR WHO DINOSAUR BOOK** (illus)	**75p**
	0426200020	**DOCTOR WHO DISCOVERS PREHISTORIC ANIMALS** (NF) (illus)	**75p**
	0426200039	**DOCTOR WHO DISCOVERS SPACE TRAVEL** (NF) (illus)	**75p**
	0426200047	**DOCTOR WHO DISCOVERS STRANGE AND MYSTERIOUS CREATURES** (NF) (illus)	**75p**
	042620008X	**DOCTOR WHO DISCOVERS THE STORY OF EARLY MAN** (NF) (illus)	**75p**
	0426200136	**DOCTOR WHO DISCOVERS THE CONQUERORS** (NF) (illus)	**75p**
Δ	0426200640	Terrance Dicks **JUNIOR DR WHO: THE GIANT ROBOT** (illus)	**75p**
Δ	0426115783	**DOCTOR WHO AND THE THREE DOCTORS**	**75p**
Δ	0426200233	**DOCTOR WHO AND THE TIME WARRIOR**	**75p**
Δ	0426110765	Gerry Davis **DOCTOR WHO AND THE TOMB OF THE CYBERMEN**	**75p**
Δ	0426200683	Terrance Dicks **DOCTOR WHO AND THE UNDERWORLD**	**75p**
Δ	0426200829	Malcolm Hulke **DOCTOR WHO AND THE WAR GAMES**	**75p**
Δ	0426110846	Terrance Dicks **DOCTOR WHO AND THE WEB OF FEAR**	**75p**
Δ	0426113241	Bill Strutton **DOCTOR WHO AND THE ZARBI** (illus)	**70p**
Δ	0426200675	Terrance Dicks **THE ADVENTURES OF K9 AND OTHER MECHANICAL CREATURES** (illus)	**75p**
Δ	0426200950	Terry Nation's **DALEK SPECIAL** (illus)	**95p**
Δ	0426114477	**DOCTOR WHO MONSTER BOOK** (Colour illus)	**50p**
Δ	0426200012	**THE SECOND DOCTOR WHO MONSTER BOOK** (Colour illus)	**70p**

† For sale in Britain and Ireland only.
* Not for sale in Canada. ● Reissues.
Δ Film & T.V. tie-ins.

If you enjoyed this book and would like to have information sent to you about other TARGET titles, write to the address below.

You will also receive:
A FREE TARGET BADGE!
Based on the TARGET BOOKS symbol — see front cover of this book — this attractive three-colour badge, pinned to your blazer-lapel or jumper, will excite the interest and comment of all your friends!

and you will be further entitled to:
FREE ENTRY INTO THE TARGET DRAW!
All you have to do is cut off the coupon below, write on it your name and address in *block capitals,* and pin it to your letter. Twice a year, in June, and December, coupons will be drawn 'from the hat' and the winner will receive a complete year's set of TARGET books.

Write to:

TARGET BOOKS
44 Hill Street
London W1X 8LB

cut here

Full name ....

Address..

....

....

Age.....................

PLEASE ENCLOSE A SELF-ADDRESSED STAMPED ENVELOPE WITH YOUR COUPON!